ATOLL

BY THE SAME AUTHOR

Adapted to Stress
Bitter Autumn
One Sword Less
On a Still Night
Cold Route to Freedom
Flameout
Nightdive
Hell Seed
Glimpse of Forever
Snowtrap
Firestorm
Hell's Arena

WRITING AS LINDSEY GREY

Smoke from Another Fire

ATOLL

COLIN D. PEEL

ST. MARTIN'S PRESS

NEW YORK

 For information, address St. Martin's Press, 175 Fifth Avenue, New York, N.Y. 10010.

Design by Judy C. Christensen

Library of Congress Cataloging-in-Publication Data

Peel, Colin D.
Atoll/Colin D. Peel.
p. cm.
"A Thomas Dunne book."
ISBN 0-312-07646-0
I. Title.
PR6066.E36A96 1992
823'.914—dc20 92-144
CIP

First Edition: July 1992

10 9 8 7 6 5 4 3 2 1

FOR ZAC

AUTHOR'S NOTE

Because the atoll described in this book is better known as Mururoa, I have chosen to use this spelling instead of Moruroa, which is more correct.

ATOLL

PROLOGUE

THE atoll was at peace, a ring of pure white coral floating in the deep indigo of the Pacific, a reef of almost unimaginable beauty encircling the lighter shades of blue and green of the lagoon inside it. Asleep in the warm waters of the ocean, the island was as it always had been.

Yet once there had been no island here, no coral reef and no lagoon. For like the others of the archipelago, this atoll had taken six million years to build. Since the volcanism that had marked its birth, only slowly had lava flowed upward from the seabed ten thousand feet below and not until the volcano had died and drowned did the fringing reef at last begin to grow.

With the formation of the reef came the real beginnings of the atoll, the transition from dead volcano to an island of living coral drawing its food from the South Pacific to build upon itself. Imperceptibly, over a period of a million years, the atoll became truly beautiful, a necklace of sparkling coral nearly thirty miles long, an atoll as tranquil and unspoiled as any place on earth could be.

Today, from a distance, the atoll appeared unchanged. A fringe of foam surrounded the reef, the lagoon was a lighter green near the open channels along the southern edge of the island and, where the reef plate was low enough for the sea to wash over it, a characteristic white stain had spread out over a large area of the lagoon surface. Even on the flat areas of the atoll itself there was nothing to identify the difference between today and any other day in this secluded corner of the world.

The difference lay instead unseen, hidden deep beneath the lagoon at the end of a long steel needle which had been driven into the very heart of the atoll.

Extending downward through the coral debris on the lagoon floor the needle had pierced the limestone layers, pushed aside the clay and finally penetrated the volcanic rock two thousand feet below the reef. And there, at the needle's end, in a sealed steel cylinder, two and a half feet in diameter and twenty-eight feet long, was the means by which the atoll would be changed forever.

Entombed by the six hundred tons of rocks and concrete which had been used to fill the tube above it, the bomb waited now for the signal to test its power against the foundations of the atoll.

An hour ago, in another hemisphere ten thousand miles away, four men had confirmed that the test would go ahead. The approval was not unexpected. The Direction des Centres d'Essais Nucléaires were busy on more pressing matters and predictably unwilling to question staff in Tahiti about the timing of the test. Today's test was routine—no more than one in a series of seven and, until the results were known, of little immediate interest to anyone in the Paris center.

On the atoll now, the countdown had reached a crucial stage. In several of the control buildings and in the Papeete offices of the Centre d'Expérimentation du Pacifique, technicians, scientists and engineers became more active.

Behind the airstrip, a light breeze that had been rustling the palms had died away and although someone had forgotten to switch off a compressor under one of the drilling derricks, the atoll was unusually quiet. Even the sea was calmer than it had been earlier, and spray was no longer being carried over the reef into the lagoon.

Five seconds before the countdown reached zero the compressor stopped, leaving the atoll to wait in silence.

A moment later, nearly half a mile below the reef, the

detonation began—a thermonuclear explosion of inconceivable proportions.

Traveling at fifteen miles a second, a shock wave blasted outward into the atoll, vaporizing rock with temperatures hotter than the surface of the sun. Pressures of a million atmospheres tore at the fabric of the atoll, melting the basalt, shattering and fragmenting the base of the volcano on which the island stood.

Where once the bomb had been, a cavity of white-hot molten glass began to fill with fractured rock—an avalanche of incandescent boulders wrenched from the cavern roof to create a chimney more than five hundred feet high.

Another underground nuclear test at Mururoa atoll was over. An explosion equivalent to the detonation of one hundred and fifty thousand tons of TNT had generated yet another enormous subterranean cavern that would remain radioactive for a thousand years.

At ground level there had been the familiar tremor not unlike a small earthquake and, for a while, ripples had traveled out over the lagoon. The atoll had stirred in its sleep but the disturbance had been short-lived and already on the reef there was nothing to show what had taken place so far beneath the surface.

Seventy-three times the atoll had been rocked before by similar explosions and seventy-three times the atoll had shrugged them off. With the test completed and with the radioactivity locked safely into volcanic glass two thousand feet below sea level all was well at Mururoa. Soon the computers would be busy analyzing the results from today's explosion, and soon, with the atoll once again at peace, drilling could begin for the next test.

But in the deep water outside the reef, all was far from well. Between test sites Giselle and Camélia, on the northwestern flank of the volcano, the ocean had already searched out the first major crack in the atoll's structure. And, not long from now, hot radioactive brine from flooded caverns would start its slow journey upward into the lagoon.

ONE

—1990—

THE rain was sweeping across the parking lot in great sheets, blurring Carlisle's view of the university and hammering on the car roof so hard that he could barely hear the radio.

He switched the radio off. The weather forecast had said rain and there was rain, and it was no use sitting here hoping it might just ease long enough for him to dash across to the building. In Honolulu, when it started raining like this, Carlisle knew you could either ignore it or enjoy it. This morning he decided it might be quite refreshing.

Making no attempt to hurry, he opened the car door and stepped out into the warm Hawaiian rain. A few moments later he arrived at his office on the third floor and stood dripping in the doorway.

"Goodness." His secretary stared at him. "How far away did you have to park?"

"Over on the east side. It wouldn't have made any difference where I parked. I got this wet locking the car door." Carlisle grinned at her. "Stop looking so disapproving. My official university meeting suit is in the office and I've got another shirt somewhere."

"The suit might be a good idea. I don't think wet shorts are quite right for your image this morning. You have a visitor."

"I do?" Carlisle was surprised.

Stephanie Tyrrel stood up from her desk. "Give me your briefcase, get your suit and go and change."

Carlisle maintained his grip on the case. "Who is it?"

Stephanie sighed. "You are making a puddle on the floor and I'm not going to tell you anything unless you at least make some effort to look as though you work here."

"I don't work here." Carlisle released his case. "I'm a visiting geologist—remember?"

"Well, today you're a visiting geologist with a visitor. He's been waiting over an hour for you. I've put him in the empty office along the hall and given him coffee."

"Okay." Carlisle went to collect his suit and dry shirt from the office, and headed off to the washroom.

When he returned, Stephanie inspected him more closely. She frowned. "John, what exactly have you done to your hair?"

"I put it under one of those hot-air hand drier things in the toilet. Why?"

"It's all standing on end." She started reaching out, intending to smooth it down but stopped herself in time. "Here." She handed him a business card. "Your visitor is a Mr. Tumahai. He's Polynesian, tall, well dressed and around fifty-five. He speaks English with a slight accent and he's a very polite man."

There was nothing on the card to say who Mr. Tumahai might be or where he was from. Carlisle put the card on his desk and tried to remember if he had heard the name before.

"Is he Hawaiian?" he asked. "Japanese Hawaiian?"

Stephanie shook her head. "I don't think so. Why don't I just go and get him?"

"All right." Carlisle transferred a pile of books from his

desk to the floor and stuffed a number of files into the gap between the filing cabinet and the wall. He was still clearing up when Stephanie accompanied his visitor into the office.

"Mr. Tumahai." Carlisle put out his hand. "Good morning."

"You are Mr. John Carlisle from England?" Tumahai was a distinguished-looking man with dark hair and bushy white eyebrows. He shook hands firmly, clasping his hat to his chest as he did so.

"Scotland," Carlisle said. "I was born there but that was a long time ago. I'm not sure where I'm from anymore."

Tumahai smiled slightly. "Nowadays it is more important how a man thinks, not where he comes from." He continued holding his hat and made no attempt to move farther into the room.

"Please come and sit down." Carlisle couldn't pick the accent but Tumahai certainly wasn't a Hawaiian. His English had a more precise European edge to it and his manner was not that of an American.

"Mr. Tumahai." Stephanie spoke from the door as she was leaving. "Can I get you some more coffee?"

"No, thank you. You have already been very kind." Tumahai sat down.

"I won't either, thanks, Steph." Carlisle slid over another chair and joined his visitor on the same side of the desk.

"It is kind of you to see me," Tumahai said. "May I put my hat on your desk—even though it is a little damp?"

"Sure." Carlisle was intrigued by the hat. Woven from strips of what appeared to be bleached palm leaves, it was unlike any hat he had seen before.

"I think it will be best if I waste as little of your time as possible." Tumahai looked directly at Carlisle. "Because it is necessary for me to present my case as clearly as possible, please forgive me if I am too forthright."

"Fine. What can I do for you?"

"It is more a question of what you may be able to do for others rather than for me, Mr. Carlisle. Before I begin I should like to apologize for not writing to you or perhaps telephoning for an appointment. I have friends who recommended I approach you directly without first making you aware of my business."

"Why did your friends think that?"

"Because what I have to ask you is very difficult. I hope that by coming here I may persuade you. An inquiry by letter or by telephone would, I think, not have captured your interest or gained your sympathy."

Carlisle began to speak but stopped when Tumahai held up his hand.

"Please. I believe I can answer your questions before you ask them." Tumahai straightened in his chair. "My name you know. What you have not yet been able to discover is exactly who I am or where I have come from. So, I shall tell you at once. I am a politician—or a politician of a kind. And I am from French Polynesia, from the islands of Tahiti."

"You've come all the way from Tahiti to see me?" Carlisle was genuinely astonished.

"Yesterday I have flown from Papeete here to Honolulu. It is a long journey but, I hope, one which will be worthwhile."

"I don't understand." Carlisle paused. "I mean, why have you come to see me?"

"Because you are a geologist. Because you are here to study the hydrology of the Hawaiian islands—because you are an expert on submarine shield volcanoes. You have published many papers on the subject, Mr. Carlisle. Some I have read, although I confess my comprehension of them is less than I would like it to be."

Carlisle didn't say anything.

"It is very simple. I am here to ask if you will work for the people of French Polynesia." Tumahai spoke more quietly.

"To see if you will help us in a small but important way."

By now Carlisle knew what was coming, knew why Tumahai was sitting here in his office. "Mururoa," he said. "It's about the atoll, isn't it?"

Tumahai nodded. "Indeed. Not a difficult guess for you to make, I think."

"No." Carlisle stood up. "I'm afraid you may have come all this way for nothing, though."

"I have considered that possibility with great care, Mr. Carlisle. But, before you reach any judgment, I am counting on your willingness to hear me out. Will you extend that courtesy to me?"

"Of course." Carlisle was uneasy. "I just don't think I can help you, that's all. I'm here in Hawaii for two years to study the volcanics of the Kilauea volcano on the big island. That's what I do for a living. I don't suppose I'm any different from anyone else who's thought about nuclear testing in the Pacific but I'm a geologist, not a politician."

"You do not approve of what the French are doing at Mururoa?"

"No, not particularly." Carlisle met Tumahai's eyes. "I think there are good arguments for and against nuclear weapons in this rotten world we live in, but I don't support the idea of any country testing its weapon systems in someone else's backyard."

"And do you also believe nuclear testing in the Pacific is dangerous, Mr. Carlisle?"

"In what way?"

"For the people of French Polynesia—for all the people of the South Pacific."

"I don't know." Carlisle's answer was deliberately evasive. Tumahai's remarks were becoming increasingly dramatic and Carlisle wanted to avoid encouraging him any further.

"Then let me see if I can help you arrive at an opinion. I am more than happy to stand up also while I explain, but perhaps we would both be more comfortable if you were to return to your chair."

Carlisle made himself relax. "I'm sorry." He sat down again facing Tumahai. "I just don't want to get mixed up in any discussion on the philosophy of nuclear testing. I'm sure you're a very persuasive person but it's not my scene, Mr. Tumahai—not as a geologist, not as an environmentalist, not as anything. Anyway I really don't know a hell of a lot about hydrogen bombs."

"Nor do I." Tumahai cleared his throat. "And, unlike you, I also know nothing of geology. That, however, is not a barrier to understanding what is happening at Mururoa."

"Okay, I'm listening." Carlisle smiled. "It mightn't look like it but I'm usually pretty good at listening."

"I shall not bore you with the history of the French occupation of Tahiti—it is a separate issue, tragic enough but nothing to do with what I am about to tell you. It is the French tests which I will explain. You see, Mr. Carlisle, since July 1976 there have been seventy-four subsurface detonations of nuclear devices at Mururoa atoll. Before that, a large number of atmospheric tests were carried out above the lagoon but it is the underground tests that have become the major concern to some of us who live in French Polynesia."

"Because you're worried about radioactive contamination?" Carlisle interrupted.

"That is a very wide term." For the first time since his arrival in the office Tumahai appeared impatient.

"Go on," Carlisle said.

"Until 1984 all of the bombs were exploded under the reef itself at depths between five hundred and twelve hundred meters, but more recently the tests have been carried out beneath the floor of the lagoon. There are several reasons for this. One is that the French are running out of sites along the reef. Another is that the reef has subsided in several places and is now submerged as a result of the testing program."

"Is the reef cracked?" Carlisle asked. "I remember reading about the possibility of the limestone being cracked somewhere."

Tumahai nodded. "As well as cracks in the coral there are indeed cracks in the limestone beneath the reef. However, as you will appreciate, Mr. Carlisle, the coral is not very strong and even though it is fractured there is no real danger from any leakage of radioactivity."

"Because you mean the bombs are exploded much lower down in the atoll," Carlisle said. "Inside the volcanic rock."

"That is correct. Each explosion creates a large cavern in the basalt rock. Immediately after a bomb has been detonated, molten and semimolten rock flows into these caverns, trapping most of the radioactive material. This kind of rock, as you know, is high in silica and is said to encase nearly two thirds of all radioactive compounds inside it once it has cooled to become volcanic glass."

"How big are these caverns?" Carlisle's interest was growing.

"They are very large—depending on the size of the explosion and the depth at which it occurs. A one hundred kiloton warhead exploded at a depth of one thousand meters produces a cavern eighty meters in diameter with a chimney above it around two hundred meters high. These are figures which have secretly been obtained from the French."

"Christ!" Carlisle tried to visualize a cavern of that size, half a mile inside the atoll.

"You are surprised?" Tumahai asked.

"Yes, I am. It's hard to imagine anything powerful enough to do that sort of damage."

"What I would like you to imagine, Mr. Carlisle, is the seawater that very slowly flows through the atoll into these caverns. The rock is, of course, slightly porous and it is certain the caverns eventually fill with water."

"Then what happens?" Carlisle asked.

"According to the French authorities, nothing." Tumahai smiled. "The water is said to seep through the atoll at a rate of only one meter per year."

"That's probably right. It's nearly the same rate as the water moves through the volcanics here in Hawaii."

"But of course it will travel more quickly if the base rock is fractured or cracked," Tumahai said quietly. "And once seawater enters the caverns it will become a hot brine that will try to rise to the surface."

Carlisle stared at him. "Hot brine attacks volcanic glass, did you know that?"

"I have been told. I have also learned that even though the brine will become radioactive by dissolving the glass, it will never reach the surface because of the layer of clay between the volcanic rock and the limestone layer above it."

"Mm. Maybe." Carlisle wasn't sure. "Mr. Tumahai, are you telling me the atoll is cracked? Deep down, I mean."

"We are not certain. However, we do know the clay layer has been compressed to almost nothing in places because of the explosions. That is why parts of the reef have sunk. We believe that the chimney of one cavern no longer has a clay layer above it at all. The cork, so to speak, has been withdrawn from the bottle."

Carlisle had the picture clearly now. "So if the atoll's cracked you're worried about radioactive brine spewing upward into the lagoon from one of the caverns," he said.

"And subsequently out into the Pacific, Mr. Carlisle."

"But the whole thing's a guess, isn't it? Or do you know for sure that's what's happening?"

"The French atomic energy commission has prepared estimates of leakage rates and have taken many core samples of rock from special drill holes. They have issued official statements saying it will be five hundred to a thousand years before the first traces of underground water appear in the lagoon."

"You didn't answer my question," Carlisle said gently.

"I cannot answer it. But I can tell you the French have recently become extremely worried and very secretive. On Mururoa at this moment there is more activity than there has been for some time. Heavy equipment is arriving weekly from France and the CEP are recruiting specialist staff from many different places."

"What's the CEP?" Carlisle asked.

"The Centre d'Expérimentation du Pacifique. They control everything on the atoll."

Carlisle looked at him. "So what do you think's going on?"

"The nature of the equipment which is being delivered leads us to believe the French are making ready to force high-pressure concrete into one of the underground caverns. We think they are trying to prevent seawater from flowing into it."

"Because you think the atoll's cracked open three thousand feet under water?"

Tumahai smiled again. "Or one thousand meters. Yes. And because the clay layer is now too thin to stop contaminated water from escaping upward."

"I see." Carlisle was thinking hard. If Tumahai was right—if cracks really had started opening up in the base of the atoll—hot seawater would certainly percolate up through the rock whether the rock was fractured or not. But even hot water would travel very slowly and it was unlikely that the clay layer would have disappeared completely.

"You haven't any proof of this, have you?" Carlisle said.

"We have people on the atoll who have smuggled Geiger counters onto some barges in the lagoon. In the last month there has been a rise in radioactivity but I cannot tell you how much. I have difficulty in understanding such things."

"Who's 'we'?"

"Mr. Carlisle, there are many people in French Polynesia who have spent their lives trying to stop these nuclear tests. Some are Tahitians, some are Chinese, some are French. There is, or there was, the Front de Libération de la Polynésie. There is the Autonomie Interne, which is an organization for Tahitian self-government, and a number of other similar institutions. For the purpose of our conversation here today I can say I represent the interests of all people who wish to bring an end to the testing program and an end to the French occupation of our islands." Tumahai smiled. "There, I have made the speech I had promised I would avoid."

Carlisle grinned. "I thought it sounded pretty good."

"Ah, but I would do better in French." Tumahai hesitated. "Have I explained to you what I believe is happening at Mururoa in a clear manner?"

"Yes, you have. I'm not sure why you've told me, though. I can't give you an opinion on the likelihood of radioactive water leaking into the lagoon. Except for what I've read about it and what you've said this morning, I don't know very much about the geology of Mururoa atoll."

"If you could examine the core samples which have been brought out from the drill holes near the cavern, could you determine the degree of fracturing or porosity in the rock surrounding it?"

Carlisle nodded. "Probably."

"And could you establish whether or not the clay layer has been destroyed?"

"As long as there are enough samples from each side of the layer or where the layer used to be." Carlisle stopped. "Have you got the samples?"

"No, Mr. Carlisle. I wish we did. You must understand they are stored on the atoll under very tight security."

"Then I don't think I can help you." Carlisle had not

intended to sound quite so emphatic. "Look, I really am sorry."

"You do not understand," Tumahai said. "I have not come to seek an opinion from you here in Hawaii. I have come to ask if you would return to Tahiti with me."

"To Mururoa?"

"Yes."

"Mr. Tumahai, I can't. I've already told you. I'm working on a research project here." Carlisle was uneasy again. "It's got nothing to do with how I feel about what's going on at Mururoa. I have the greatest sympathy for the Tahitians but I can't get mixed up in what you're trying to do."

"And what is it you believe I am doing, Mr. Carlisle?"

"I imagine you're trying to get some kind of hard geological evidence to prove your theory about radioactive water leaking into the lagoon. If you could do that you'd probably be able to bring a fair bit of pressure to bear on the French to stop the tests." Carlisle paused. "World opinion is hardly on their side as it is. I don't think it'd take much publicity to make them pack up and go home. That's your game plan, isn't it?"

"Put very simply, yes. Unfortunately the evidence must be collected soon—before the high-pressure concrete is pumped into the ground. Once that is done, natural flushing of the lagoon will quickly reduce the level of radioactivity in the water." Tumahai looked directly at Carlisle. "I was hoping you would agree to come to Tahiti."

"It wouldn't be any help if I did," Carlisle said. "I'd need to have a good look at the atoll and see the core samples."

"Both can be arranged, Mr. Carlisle. We also have another plan to obtain information. Through our friends in France we have been able to obtain some very clever and very small electronic sensors—transducers I believe they are called. We intend to put these secretly into the liquid concrete as it is pumped into the cavern. They will provide us with data on rock temperature and the level of radioactivity at different depths in the atoll."

"It's not my kind of thing, Mr. Tumahai. I'm afraid you're going to have to find someone else." Carlisle left his chair and went to the window. Outside it was still raining but not so hard.

"We are prepared to pay you one hundred and fifty thousand American dollars for your trouble."

Carlisle swung around. "I don't want your money. I just don't want to be involved. I'm sorry, but that's how it is. You've got the wrong guy."

"I do not think so. I think we have the right man but I have failed in my efforts to persuade you. It is my fault." Tumahai joined Carlisle at the window. "I too am sorry."

"There are other geologists. I still don't know why you chose me."

"Because of your reputation. There are few people who have studied submarine shield volcanoes in such detail and it was thought you would respond favorably to our request. We have examined your background rather thoroughly, Mr. Carlisle."

"Did you think I'd do it for the money?"

"No." Tumahai smiled. "According to our assessment, you are not a man who is motivated by money nor by sexual gratification or power."

"Really." Carlisle didn't like the idea of someone poking around trying to build up a psychological profile of him. "Makes me sound kind of boring, doesn't it?"

"Is there anything else I can say?" Tumahai asked.

"No." Carlisle sat down on the windowsill.

"It would take less than a week for you to undertake the assignment in Tahiti. You could be back here to study your Kilauea in very little time."

"Yes, I know. But the answer's still no. There's no point looking for the right weak spot, Mr. Tumahai. I'm sure there are plenty of them outside power, sex and money, but you've got the big ones covered so you're wasting your time."

Tumahai retrieved his hat from the table. "You are a strong-willed young man, Mr. Carlisle. I have enjoyed meeting with you."

"Are you going back to Tahiti today?"

"I think not. There is another matter I must attend to. Tomorrow, perhaps. I will see."

Carlisle levered himself off the windowsill. "I'll ask my secretary to get you a taxi. It's pretty wet out there."

"Thank you, but I have a car and driver waiting." Tumahai shook hands. "Do you enjoy living in Hawaii, Mr. Carlisle?"

"Very much."

"Then one day you must visit Tahiti. In many ways it is not dissimilar. I would be pleased and flattered if you would accept an invitation to stay in my home should you ever come to the South Pacific."

"Thank you. I'll remember that." Carlisle accompanied Tumahai to the door where he said goodbye.

Stephanie came into the office as soon as Tumahai had gone. "So who was he?" she asked.

"Daniel Tumahai."

"I know that. I mean what did he want?"

Carlisle told her.

It was nearly five o'clock when Carlisle left the university. The rain had slackened to a drizzle but the afternoon had become unpleasantly warm, making him feel sticky in his suit.

Once in his car, he pushed the air-conditioning control to Cold and waited for the mist to clear from the windshield before he started his journey home.

Several minutes later, with the temperature and humidity at a more comfortable level, the car was still in the parking lot with Carlisle motionless behind the wheel. Having wasted half the afternoon in the library and the other half reading at his desk, John Carlisle was too angry and too preoccupied to drive.

His annoyance was with himself—a sense of irritation that had been with him ever since Tumahai had left this morning. Most of the books in the university library had told him little he did not already know about the geology of atolls. The volcanism that had formed the islands of French Polynesia was nearly identical to the geological processes he was studying in Hawaii and, apart from checking on the likely thickness of the clay layer at Mururoa, Carlisle had not bothered to read the books in any detail.

He had gone to the library unwillingly in the first place, knowing there were other more important things he should be doing. As a result, he was not altogether surprised when his interest had drifted away from geology, turning instead to what Tumahai had said about the history of nuclear testing on the atoll.

Even then Carlisle had not been sure what was causing his irritation. The feeling had persisted until he'd left the building and got into his car. Only now was it beginning to go.

It was the whole damn thing, Carlisle decided. The assumption that he would want to get involved, the intrusion into his private life by a stranger looking for some psychological flaw in his character, and then the offer of money by someone he had never met before. If the French had been stupid or careless enough to let radioactive brine leak into the lagoon, the French could clean it up. And if someone like Daniel Tumahai could find a way to stop bombs from being exploded in the Pacific, that was fine—just as long as it was someone else. Carlisle had other things to do and other things to think about.

He switched on the windshield wipers and swung the nose of his car out onto the road.

As an academic exercise, the afternoon had perhaps not been entirely wasted. He had found a useful reference on basalt faulting and he already felt less guilty about the rather offhand way he had treated Tumahai's proposal. There was no other sensible reply he could have given. He had known it then and four hours' thinking had contributed nothing to make him reconsider.

Although the traffic was crawling because of the weather, and made worse by an accident on the Lunalilo Freeway at Kalihi, Carlisle spent no more time worrying about Mururoa atoll or about Daniel Tumahai.

Entering his apartment, he went directly to the bedroom where he took off his shoes and exchanged his suit for an old pair of shorts.

He was taking a can of beer from the fridge when the phone rang. It was Stephanie.

"Hi." Carlisle opened the can with one hand.

"You left your briefcase at the office."

"It's okay. I'm not doing any work tonight."

"I've got it here at home with me. I can bring it around if you want."

Lately Carlisle had begun to wonder about Stephanie. By being almost excessively cool and professional on some days and embarrassingly friendly to him on others she made him never quite certain how to treat her. This confusion had not concerned him greatly, but more recently, in the last few weeks, he had found himself thinking about her at home.

"Thanks for the offer but I really don't need the case." He tried to sound firm.

"I think you might. There's something for you inside it."

Carlisle sighed. "Steph, stop being mysterious. I'm too tired. What do you mean?"

"A courier brought a package for you—just after you'd gone."

"What kind of package?"

"I don't know. I haven't opened it. I just stuck it in your case and brought it home. It looks like a book or something."

"I'm not expecting anything. I'll see what it is tomorrow."

"Look, I have to go out anyway. I'll drop it off at your apartment. It's no trouble. I'll be there in twenty minutes."

Carlisle replaced the receiver, unable to decide whether he was pleased or not. He went to find a cleaner pair of shorts, then started to clear up the kitchen and the living room.

He was still busy when Stephanie arrived. To his surprise she was wearing an expensive-looking sleeveless dress and white high-heeled shoes.

Trying not to stare, Carlisle asked her in. When he had first met Stephanie he had found her attractive enough, but in the ten months she had worked for him, he'd always been careful to maintain what he believed was the correct kind of relationship between them. Seeing her now, dressed like this with her hair loose, Carlisle thought he had either been unusually dumb or that he had failed to understand the signals.

"Is something the matter?" Stephanie handed him the briefcase.

"No. I'm not used to seeing you in those sort of clothes. You look different."

"Oh." She smiled. "If that's a compliment—thank you."

"I didn't say it very well, did I?" He grinned at her. "You look great. Can I offer you a beer? It's all I've got."

"Beer's fine." She sat down. "Are you going to open the parcel?"

"In a minute." Carlisle went to the kitchen and poured the contents of a beer can into a glass. By the time he returned he was fairly sure he would ask her out to dinner.

He handed her the glass.

"Thank you." She glanced up at him. "You didn't want me to come, did you?"

He took the parcel out of the briefcase. "I didn't mean to sound rude on the phone."

"It's okay. I'll go when I've had my drink."

Carlisle decided. "Steph, could I take you out to dinner?"

"For bringing your case over?"

"No, but we can make that the excuse if you like."

She smiled again. "I'd love to but I can't tonight. I told you when I phoned I was going out." By declining his invitation and sensing his disappointment, Stephanie was now more sure. "I'm not doing anything tomorrow."

"Right." He brightened. "If it's not raining we'll go somewhere nice." He opened one end of the parcel and withdrew a sheaf of paper and a number of photographs.

"Dirty pictures in a plain brown wrapper?" Stephanie sipped her beer.

Carlisle didn't answer her.

"John, what are they?"

"Oh Christ," Carlisle muttered.

She stood up and came to see. Quickly he tried to slide the photos back inside the parcel. He fumbled, dropping two of them faceup on the carpet in front of her.

For a moment Stephanie stared at them. Then she looked away. "My God," she said quietly. "They're from that man Tumahai who came to see you, aren't they? I should've guessed."

"And I should've realized he gave up too easily." He gathered the photos from the floor. "You don't want to see these again, do you?"

She shook her head.

Each of the photographs Carlisle was holding showed women lying on their backs with their legs apart in the obstetric ward of a hospital. Women who had just given birth to what should have been babies. Instead, they had given birth to shapeless bags of bloodstained jelly.

Typewritten headings on both photos gave the date and the name of the hospital. On the bottom, in black ink, someone had written, "Live, full-term, mutant fetus of the French Polynesian jellybaby type."

Carlisle laid the photographs on the table, covering them with the other documents Tumahai had sent.

"I'd better go." Stephanie went to the door. "You've got some heavy reading to do by the look of it."

"Damn the man," Carlisle said.

"He still thinks he can make you change your mind."

"Well, he's bloody wrong."

Stephanie turned in the doorway. "I'll see you tomorrow. And thank you for asking me to dinner." She paused. "I think it's about time, don't you?"

Carlisle could smell her perfume. "It's my fault. Scottish geologists are pretty slow kind of people." He grinned. "We're okay once we get going, though."

After he had walked her to her car and said goodbye, he returned to the apartment and opened another can of beer. Trying to decide whether or not he should examine the documents from Tumahai had brought back the feeling of irritation, this time mixed up with his thoughts about Stephanie.

The whole day had been a mix-up, Carlisle thought. The rain, Tumahai, Stephanie and now these sickening photos Tumahai had sent.

Leaving the photographs on the table, Carlisle picked up one of the documents and began to read.

At midnight, five beer cans later and mentally numb, he tore each of the documents in half, then systematically ripped the photographs to pieces before he went to bed.

The gesture was unsuccessful. Still awake at three in the morning, Carlisle reached for his phone to call Zac Brennan.

TWO

CARLISLE had not expected Tumahai to be so early. Shredded paper lay everywhere and empty beer cans from the night before were littered from one end of the apartment to the other.

"Please come in." Carlisle inspected his watch. "I'm sorry the place is such a mess."

"You omitted to say a time when you telephoned so I was not certain when I should come." Tumahai removed his hat. "If it is inconvenient I can return later." His eyes flickered over the pieces of photographs on the carpet.

"Just ignore how it looks in here." Carlisle grinned. "It's not normally quite this bad."

"You have destroyed all of the material I sent you?"

"Pretty much," Carlisle said cheerfully.

"But you have nevertheless changed your mind?"

"No, I didn't say that. I asked you over for breakfast because I have an idea that might interest you."

"Then I have misinterpreted your phone call."

"I thought you would." Carlisle had seen Tumahai's expression change. "I've got eggs, bacon and coffee. Or we can go out somewhere if you'd rather do that."

"Just a cup of coffee, I think." Tumahai followed Carlisle into the kitchen. "Why precisely did you telephone me, Mr. Carlisle?"

Carlisle put bread in the toaster and poured two cups of coffee from the percolator. "It's a bit complicated," he said. "But don't get the idea I've changed my mind about going to Tahiti. I haven't."

"Did you study the statistics on the high incidence of cancer and birth defects in French Polynesia from the information I provided?"

Carlisle nodded.

"And did you also examine the report on the 1981 cyclone that swept several kilograms of toxic plutonium waste into the lagoon? People were permitted to swim in the lagoon almost immediately afterward—did you read that, Mr. Carlisle?"

"I read everything," Carlisle said. "I know all about small, contaminated fish from the lagoon being eaten by tuna and bonito outside the reef. I know two thousand tons of locally caught fish are sold in the Papeete market every year and I know that if I lived in Tahiti I'd be as worried as hell even if the atoll isn't cracked."

"I see. But you are nevertheless still not prepared to help in any way?"

After spreading butter on one piece of toast and marmalade on the other, Carlisle put them together to make a sandwich. "I think someone else can help you more than I can," he said.

"Like you, he is a geologist? A colleague of yours?"

"No." Carlisle shook his head. "He's a mining engineer."

"Then he is not the man I am looking for."

"How do you know?" Carlisle said. "You've never met him. You don't know a damn thing about him."

Tumahai sat down and drank some of his coffee. "I am

sorry. Please explain how someone who is not a geologist could be of any assistance at Mururoa."

"You don't need a geologist. All you want is someone who's able to read the core samples you say the French have got hidden on the atoll." Carlisle paused. "And someone who can sniff around to find out why the French have suddenly decided to pump concrete into one of the caverns."

"And your mining engineer can do these things?"

"Yes, he can."

Tumahai studied his coffee cup. "Do I understand it is your recommendation that I ask him?"

"I've already asked him. I phoned him last night."

"Why should this man offer his help?" Tumahai looked up. "A man I have not met or spoken to?"

"For the money."

"Ah." Tumahai frowned. "It is a very bad reason."

"Maybe. It depends on the kind of person you're getting for your money. Zac Brennan's psychological profile might not be the same as mine but he'd do a good job for you."

"This Mr. Brennan, he is also English?" Tumahai corrected himself. "Scottish?"

"No." Carlisle smiled. "Don't I remember something about it being more important how a man thinks than where he comes from?"

"But I would like to know," Tumahai said politely.

"Zac's an American."

"And he is a friend of yours?"

"He does a lot of work for me on the Big Island."

Tumahai's face was expressionless. He had placed both hands palms down on the kitchen table and appeared to be thinking.

"Mr. Carlisle, are you recommending Mr. Brennan because you are truly sympathetic to the problems of French Polynesia, or is it that you wish to assist a business acquaintance who will perhaps later give you some of the money for your trouble?"

Carlisle controlled his annoyance. "Now you listen, Mr. Tumahai," he said. "I didn't ask you to come and see me yesterday and I didn't want to spend the afternoon and half the bloody night thinking about what you'd said and reading those sick reports of yours. But I did anyway and because of that I've tried to think of some way of giving you a hand. If you don't want my help or if you don't trust me, that's fine. Go and find someone you do trust." He paused. "Making smart remarks about backhanders isn't going to get you very far with me and it sure as hell won't get you anywhere with Zac Brennan."

One of Tumahai's eyes was twitching slightly. Several seconds passed before he spoke. "I do not know what to say. You have been kind enough to listen to me and generous enough to spend a good deal of your time considering my request. I have repaid you by being rude and by abusing your hospitality. How may I apologize?"

Carlisle's irritation had been short-lived. Tumahai's manner made it easy to underestimate him.

"Well," Carlisle said. "How about this? Go ahead and apologize if you like, but I happen to think you might have been trying me out to see how I'd react. Some of the big international companies I've worked for play the same sort of games."

"You are no longer angry?"

Carlisle finished his toast. "Should I be?"

"I think not." Tumahai smiled very slightly. "Would you please tell me how I may talk to Mr. Brennan? I shall see him today if that is possible."

"I've booked us on a flight at ten thirty this morning," Carlisle said.

"You will accompany me?" Tumahai was surprised. "And Mr. Brennan is not here on Oahu?"

"Zac lives on Maui. He's got an office there. He works

over all the islands so it doesn't matter much where he lives. I'm supposed to be collecting some lava samples from him sometime this week so I might just as well go with you this morning. He's more likely to listen to what you have to say if I introduce you."

"I was under the impression he had already agreed."

Carlisle grinned. "I said I'd asked him. The hundred and fifty grand has him interested, but the rest is up to you."

"I see. But you believe he is willing to consider my proposal?"

"Oh yes, Mr. Tumahai. You can bet on it."

"Then there is one more thing, Mr. Carlisle." Tumahai was smiling again.

"Something you haven't told me?"

"No, no. I was simply going to ask if your offer of breakfast was still open. I left my hotel rather early."

"Coming up," Carlisle said. "As long as I can talk and cook at the same time I'll give you a rundown on Zac. There are a few things it might be handy to know before you meet him."

There were more people at the Kahului airport than Carlisle had seen for a while. He guided Tumahai across the building, wondering if Maui's tourist season was starting early or whether it was just that yesterday's rain had driven everyone off Oahu.

At the pick-up area outside the terminal he searched for Brennan's car among the taxis.

"Mr. Brennan will come to collect us?" Tumahai inquired.

"I asked him to." Carlisle glanced at his watch. "We're a few minutes early and Zac's usually late."

He had barely finished speaking when a red jeep pulled up and double-parked in front of them. The dents in the side and the complete absence of a top identified it to Carlisle at once.

Brennan waved.

Instructing Tumahai to follow, Carlisle navigated his way through the crush of people and cars.

"Morning," Brennan greeted him. "I'm not late, am I?" He was unshaven and wearing a bright Hawaiian shirt with holes in it. "Where's your friend?"

"Here." Carlisle introduced the Tahitian and waited while they shook hands.

Brennan started retrieving cans of diesel oil from the floor of the jeep, tossing them into the back. "I'm sorry about the transport," he said. "If you'd like to sit up here alongside me, Mr. Tumahai, John can stand up behind and hang on to the roll bar."

"Have we very far to go?" Tumahai asked. He climbed into the passenger seat.

"Wailuku," Brennan said. "Just down the road. About six and a half miles."

"Where's your car, Zac?" Carlisle asked.

"Eva's got it. She was late getting back. I figured it'd be better to come in this rather than keeping you waiting here." Brennan grinned. "Don't say it. I know this is not the good impression I'm supposed to be making."

At the curb, the boxed-in driver of a limousine was leaning on his horn.

"Hold on a second." Brennan jumped out and went over to the car where he exchanged words briefly with the driver. After bringing his fist down hard on the roof, he returned.

Standing amid the rubbish in the back of the jeep with both hands gripping the roll bar, Carlisle could not help laughing. So far, the only impression Zac had created was the one he always created. There was never any detectable variation. Whatever the circumstances, Zac Brennan was Zac Brennan.

Once they were moving and the congestion outside the

terminal had been left behind, the drive to Wailuku took only a few minutes, yet by the time the jeep pulled into Brennan's yard, Tumahai, still with one hand on his hat, was already chatting freely.

"John knows what it's like up there," Brennan said. He switched off the engine.

"Where?" Carlisle queried. From his position in the back he had not been participating in the conversation.

"I was telling Mr. Tumahai about Alberta. He asked me what a mining engineer is doing in Hawaii."

"Not a lot," Carlisle said. He had heard the story before.

"Four wasted years," Brennan said. "If those guys in Alberta had any sense they'd leave the goddamn oil in the sand. You can't drill it out and you can't suck it out."

"So you came here to Hawaii for the climate?" Tumahai said. "Because it was too cold for your kind of work in Canada?"

"Partly that." Brennan swung his legs out of the jeep. "There are a few other reasons, money not being one of them. You can make big bucks in Canada but I can tell you, Mr. Tumahai, there are times up there when you don't worry about your balls freezing off because you don't know you've got any."

"Then I think Hawaii or perhaps Tahiti is a better place for you to live, Mr. Brennan."

"Better places to live, harder places to make a living." Brennan smiled. "Not that I've ever been to Tahiti. Come on upstairs into the office where it's cooler."

Consisting of a room with unfinished walls and a toilet, built over a corrugated iron workshop, Brennan's office contained a desk, two chairs, a number of broken drilling heads and a fridge. Protruding through one wall of the office was a large air-conditioning unit with a wire cage standing on it. In the cage was a mongoose.

Carlisle went to look.

"That's Charlie," Brennan said. "Got him on the Big

Island last week. Eva reckoned there were rats in the workshop."

"Were there?" Carlisle asked.

"I don't know." Brennan grinned. "There aren't any now—not since we let Charlie loose down there at night."

Carlisle returned to the door. "If you've got those lava samples somewhere I'll go and check them out while you talk to Mr. Tumahai. I might have a drive around, too, if you don't mind me borrowing the jeep."

"You do not wish to stay, Mr. Carlisle?" Tumahai asked.

"No, I don't think so. I told Zac what I feel about things when I phoned last night. I'll be back around one o'clock."

"Here." Brennan threw him the keys to the jeep. "It jumps out of first gear. The lava's under the bench over by the big rig. If you see Eva tell her we'd like some coffee or something."

"All right." Carlisle glanced at Tumahai. "Just tell Zac what you told me about the atoll." He let himself out of the office and made his way down the outside stairs. In places, where the steel handrail was exposed to the sun it was too hot to touch, and heat was shimmering off the walls of the building in waves.

Brennan's car was standing in the yard beside the jeep. One headlight was missing and there was a deep scratch on the driver's door.

"Aloha, Mr. Carlisle," Eva shouted to him from the workshop.

Eva was a stout Hawaiian lady whose breasts seemed in perpetual danger of bursting from her dress. Today, because the dress was smaller than usual or perhaps because her breasts were larger than Carlisle remembered them, the danger appeared to be extreme. She worked for Brennan as secretary, hired hand, mother and caretaker. Carlisle was never certain which role Eva was filling on any particular day and had never been brave enough to ask.

"Hello, Eva." He walked over to her.

"We've got those rocks for you, Mr. Carlisle."

"So I hear." Wandering over to the drilling rig, Carlisle searched underneath one of the benches until he found them. "Zac said he'd like some coffee for his visitor. They're upstairs."

"Sure. What about you, Mr. Carlisle?"

"No thanks. I'll just have a look at these." He was beginning to sweat. Even with the doors open, the temperature inside the workshop was unbearable and, because his mind was more on the conversation taking place in the upstairs office than it was on the chunks of lava, he spent little time studying them.

Leaving the samples on the bench, he drifted back outside where it was cooler.

There was no doubt Brennan would take the job, Carlisle thought, if Tumahai offered it to him. Probably because he was short of cash, on the phone last night Zac hadn't even tried to disguise his interest and if Tumahai was shrewd enough to make a week or two on the atoll sound like money for nothing, Zac would jump at the opportunity.

Without deciding where he was going, Carlisle started the jeep and drove down to the Waiehu beach road where he parked in the shade beneath two palm trees.

Earlier this morning, before leaving Honolulu, he had tried to call Stephanie at the university but she had not been in her office. Although he'd left a message for her with the switchboard operator to say he'd be back in time for their dinner engagement, he wondered whether he should phone again.

He was on the point of deciding he would, when he fell asleep.

An hour later, Carlisle awoke with a thumping headache to find the jeep no longer in the shade. He drove quickly back to Wailuku, arriving at the office shortly before two. Tumahai and Brennan were in the middle of lunch. An empty wine bottle stood on the desk surrounded by the shells of several lobster tails.

"You're late," Brennan said. "I didn't know whether you were having lunch with us or not."

"It's pretty damned hot out there." Carlisle sat down on a cardboard box. "I dozed off."

"Serves you right for phoning me at some unearthly goddamn time last night," Brennan said cheerfully. "I can get Eva to fix you something if you're hungry."

"No, it's okay." Now he was out of the sun, Carlisle's headache was clearing. He changed his mind. "Maybe just a sandwich."

Brennan spoke to Eva on the phone, then put both feet on his desk and started to roll a cigarette. "Well," he said, "it's all done. As of tomorrow, if you want more holes drilled in your volcano you'll have to get someone else to do them—for a while anyway."

"You're going, then?" Carlisle was a little surprised the negotiations were over already.

"Sure." Brennan was pleased with himself.

"We may still require some assistance from you, Mr. Carlisle," Tumahai said. "Mr. Brennan is confident of his ability to analyze the core samples on the atoll but would welcome your opinion of them also. Providing we can arrange access to the samples at the right time, there may be an opportunity for him to obtain some photographs which he could bring back for you to examine."

"Fine," Carlisle said. "How's Zac getting onto the atoll to start with?"

"That is not difficult for us. We have people in Papeete and on Mururoa who are responsible for the hiring of laborers and other staff to work there."

"Friends?" Carlisle smiled.

"Indeed. There are many native Tahitians willing to assist us. However, for something as important as this we shall be very careful whom we trust. There will be no risk in landing Mr. Brennan safely on Mururoa."

Brennan lit his cigarette and puffed on it. "I'll have a real good poke around while I'm there. Whatever's going on, I don't think it'll be too hard to get a fix on it." He looked at Carlisle. "John, do you honestly believe the French could've opened up a crack in the atoll with these bombs?"

"I don't know. It may just be that one of the caverns has a higher water intake because it's in an area where the rock is particularly porous. You're probably right, though. If you keep your eyes open and ask enough questions you ought to be able to get a fair idea what's happening. It's not a very big place."

"So long as I don't ask the wrong damn people." Brennan was more thoughtful. "Be easier if my French was better. I don't know how much I remember."

"I didn't know you spoke any French at all," Carlisle said.

"There were plenty of guys from Quebec working in Alberta. I picked up a bit from them."

"Even a little French will be useful, I think," Tumahai said. "Mr. Carlisle, I am truly grateful for your introduction to Mr. Brennan. I am most pleased he has agreed to undertake this assignment."

"Well, that's good." Carlisle smiled. "All you have to do now is keep him away from all those pretty Tahitian girls."

Tumahai was amused. "In English you say 'Lock up your daughters.' Although I hardly think it necessary, I shall be sure to warn my own daughter about Mr. Brennan."

"I'm going to handle the transducer thing for them, too," Brennan said. "They need someone who can calculate the depth each transmitter will wind up at in the concrete while the stuff's being pumped."

Carlisle had half expected Tumahai would ask if Brennan would do the job. The idea of introducing electronic sensors in the concrete was ingenious and likely to provide useful information but unless the right person did it, the results could easily be meaningless. "How are you going to record the signals?" he asked.

"Mr. Tumahai has this special receiver from France." Brennan stubbed out his cigarette on a plate. "Once the concrete has carried the transducers down into the cavern and into the chimney, all I have to do is push a button. Each transducer transmits on a different frequency so it's real simple. Tumahai reckons it'll only take about five minutes to get a complete scan. I'll bring you back a copy of the chart if you want."

"Give all the copies to Mr. Tumahai," Carlisle said. "I'm sure he's got a whole bunch of hungry journalists waiting for them."

"That is correct," Tumahai said. "But it is sad, is it not? Sad that it is journalists who can stop this testing instead of scientists and politicians."

"If journalists can get the job done, use the bastards," Brennan said. "That's how the damn world works."

Eva came into the office carrying a tray. Clamping a forearm across her bosom she leaned over Carlisle to place a plate of sandwiches on the desk.

"Thanks, Eva," Carlisle said.

"You're welcome. What did you think of the rocks? Zac figured they were too small."

"No, they're fine."

"Well, that's good." She winked at Tumahai before leaving.

"What's in the sandwiches?" Brennan asked.

Carlisle inspected one. "Ham. Why?"

"Save some for Charlie. He likes ham better than he likes rats."

Carlisle ate two of the sandwiches and left the rest for the mongoose. Now that the initial discussions were over, the atmosphere in the office was remarkably relaxed, he thought. Brennan was happy, Tumahai was happy, and he himself was more than satisfied with the way things had turned out. He was especially pleased by the way Tumahai seemed to have warmed to Zac.

Anyone who didn't know Brennan usually assumed he was as ill mannered, uneducated and rough as he appeared to be. Finding out none of this was true had taken Carlisle several weeks. Tumahai, on the other hand, had either uncovered the real Brennan in a matter of hours or had decided the Brennan he'd met today was what he wanted.

Carlisle stood up and stretched. "If Eva could run me back to the airport I think I'll see if I can get on an early flight," he said. "You're booked on Hawaiian Airlines flight fifteen at six thirty, Mr. Tumahai, so you might like to stay on here and talk to Zac for a while."

"Don't worry about your friend," Brennan said. "I'll probably pack this afternoon and fly back with him to Oahu so I can get going in the morning right away."

"You are not concerned at the short notice?" Tumahai asked him.

"Hell, no." Brennan grinned. "So long as someone can fix me a seat, I'll be out of Honolulu on the same flight as you. We're going to look pretty silly if I arrive at the atoll and find they're already pumping concrete."

"Okay, I'm off." Carlisle shook hands with Tumahai. "I'm glad you didn't have to come all the way here for nothing," he said.

"I am in your debt, Mr. Carlisle. And please remember my invitation if you should one day visit Tahiti."

"I will." Carlisle started to leave. "Zac, phone me if you need anything—anything at all. I mean that." He paused with his hand on the doorknob, suddenly remembering Stephanie. "Do me a favor, will you, and call Steph at the university. Say I'm on my way. We're supposed to be going out to dinner tonight."

"Any special instructions?" Brennan grinned broadly.

"Just say I'll call her."

"Okay." Brennan waved a hand. "I'll see you when I get back."

Leaving the two men talking, Carlisle went to find Eva and organize his ride to the airport. Because it was the hottest time of day, he made a point of asking her to take him in the car.

Despite being lucky with his flight from Maui, it was past five o'clock when Carlisle arrived at his apartment. His headache was gone but he felt worn out and dirty.

Ignoring the light flashing on his answering machine, he removed his clothes and spent the next ten minutes in the shower letting the water strip away two days of heat and humidity. But the two days had been spent well enough, Carlisle decided. As a means of stopping nuclear tests at Mururoa his contribution was hardly on a grand scale, but at least he had done something. It would be interesting to see what Brennan had to say about the atoll when he got back.

He stepped from the shower, wrapped a towel round his waist and went to the answering machine.

There were two messages on it, both of them from Stephanie.

He dialed her number.

"Hi, this is Stephanie." She sounded breathless.

"It's me," Carlisle said.

"Where are you?"

"I'm at home. Didn't Zac call you?"

"Yes, but I left the messages on your machine before I heard from him. I haven't known where you've been all day."

"The girl on the switchboard at the university was supposed to let you know I was going over to Maui," Carlisle said.

"Oh." She paused. "No one told me. Am I still invited to dinner?"

"Of course. Steph, what's all this heavy breathing?"

She laughed. "I was in the shower when you called. What were you seeing Brennan about?"

"I'll explain later."

"Okay. Will you pick me up or shall I come over to your place first?"

"I'll collect you." Carlisle stopped. Besides having no idea where she lived, something in the way she asked the question made him reconsider.

"Unless you don't mind coming here," he said. "I've only just got in so I'm running a bit late."

"Is seven too early?"

"No, that's fine," Carlisle said. "I'll see you then." He rang off, wondering if he was jumping to conclusions.

Still wearing the towel, he began picking up the scattered pieces of Tumahai's reports and photographs, stuffing them into a garbage bag from the kitchen. When he'd finished, the appearance of the living room had improved, but not by very much, Carlisle had to admit. He began to work more seriously, this time using the vacuum cleaner.

When Stephanie arrived an hour and a half later, the apartment was tidier than it had been for some weeks.

"Well, good evening, Mr. Carlisle." She smiled at him. "Are we leaving right away or am I invited in?"

"Enter," Carlisle said. "I have labored greatly to make my apartment presentable for this occasion. I don't want to waste it."

Stephanie handed him a bottle wrapped in paper. "Seeing as you probably haven't had time to get anything, I brought this."

"What is it?"

"White wine." She sat down on the sofa. "I thought we could have it before we go out. It's still cold, I think."

This evening, Stephanie was wearing a white dress, gathered at the waist by a wide belt. The dress had very fine shoulder straps, which for some reason were drawing Carlisle's attention to the color and the texture of her skin.

Disturbed for the second time in two days by the way she looked, he took the bottle to the kitchen.

"You had three calls today," she shouted to him.

"Who from?"

"I don't know. They were all from the same man but he didn't leave his name. He was trying to locate your Mr. Tumahai."

Carlisle returned to the living room. "What did you say?" He gave her a glass of wine.

"The last time he phoned was around four—after I'd heard from Zac—so I just said Tumahai was on Maui seeing Brennan. Was that okay?"

"Sure." Carlisle sat down facing her. He tried to avoid looking at her ankles.

"So." She leaned back comfortably. "Where are we going?"

"Wherever you like. I haven't made any reservations."

"On purpose or because you haven't got round to it?"

Carlisle was not sure how he was supposed to interpret her remark. He said nothing.

"You don't have to take me out, you know," Stephanie said quietly. "We could get a pizza sent over. You're tired, aren't you?"

"Only because I was awake all damn night." Carlisle was drinking his wine too quickly.

"John, can I say something?"

He nodded, meeting her eyes.

"Well." She hesitated. "You and I have worked together at the university almost every day for nearly a year, haven't we?"

"Yes."

"So that means we're not exactly strangers."

He wasn't going to have to figure it out for himself after all, Carlisle realized.

"I mean, we don't have to behave as though this was a first date." She lowered her eyes.

"Steph," he said gently. "If that's the something you wanted to say, I'm not sure you did it very well."

"No. I don't think I know how to."

Intending to go over and sit beside her, Carlisle left his chair. She stood up to meet him.

A second later she was in his arms.

THREE

SINCE dawn, when he had first climbed out of bed, Brennan had been watching Papeete come alive. Now, in the street below his hotel window, swarms of people were hurrying to work or busy doing their daily shopping before the morning became too hot. European businessmen rubbed shoulders with less elegantly dressed Chinese and, everywhere, Tahitian girls with honey-colored skin and long black hair sailed past on bicycles or swung their hips along the sidewalk.

Tumahai's description of Tahiti had not been right, Brennan decided. French Polynesia was a hell of a lot more Polynesian than it was French and, apart from a few minor similarities, Tahiti was no more like Hawaii than Paris was like New York.

He left the window and turned to face the girl who was still waiting for his answer.

"Well?" Martine Tumahai had already made it clear that she neither liked nor approved of Brennan. She was a slightly built Tahitian with large eyes and a mouth that had been set firmly from the minute she had entered the room.

"Look," Brennan said. "It's easy. Your father said half now and half when I've done the job." He sat down.

"That's not what I'm talking about. Here's your check." She took an envelope from her handbag and threw it onto the table. "My father asked me to bring it. But he didn't say anything about you wanting some of it in cash."

Her English was perfect, Brennan thought. So was her figure, the pearl necklace and the expensive suit she was wearing.

"I don't think it's a very smart idea for me to go to a bank down the road and cash it here, do you?" he said.

"No."

"So why can't you or your father give me fifty grand in cash and a check for the rest of it?" Brennan said. "The rest of the first half, I mean."

She picked up the envelope. "Because, Mr. Brennan, you want American dollars and because you don't seem to realize I can't just go and withdraw that amount of foreign currency without someone wondering why I want it. Is it really so difficult for you to understand that?"

"Okay." Brennan wanted to avoid antagonizing her further. If, as he thought, she was to be his contact while he was here, there was no point in starting off like this.

"Okay what?"

"Okay, forget it." He rolled a cigarette and lit it. "You've got me wrong. You came here this morning looking for a fight because you'd already decided I was a bastard before you met me. I've got a different system. I kind of make up my mind about people after I've said hello. You don't have to like me but I'm not making your bullets for you."

"But you still want some cash?" Her eyes remained hostile.

"It'd be nice. If it's not a big hassle."

"Does it have to be in U.S. dollars?"

"No. I guess not." Brennan looked at her. "Francs are all right."

"You'll have to wait until tomorrow, then. I suppose that's a big problem for you."

"For Christ's sake stop being so damn aggressive," Brennan said. "I don't much care when I get the money. What is it with you?"

"I'll tell you what it is, Mr. Brennan. My father went to Hawaii to ask John Carlisle to help us. But instead of John Carlisle he came back with you. I don't know or care if you're a bastard. What I do know is that you're just here for the money and that means my father made a mistake."

"You never figured you might not be right?"

"In what way, Mr. Brennan?"

"Ask your father, he hired me."

Her eyes flashed. "You've already said you want the money."

"Sure," Brennan said easily. "I can use the money but that's not the only reason I'm here. You see, I happen to think your father is a pretty smart old guy who's trying to do something that needs doing. I came here because I wanted to. If this thing works out maybe it'll help a whole lot of people—not just you and your father but all those people down there in the street as well."

"Well, isn't that wonderful?" She smiled sarcastically. "An American white knight all set to save the world."

Brennan gave up. He stubbed out his cigarette wondering how much more difficult this was going to be.

"Don't worry about your money, Mr. Brennan. I'll arrange everything for you. Until then there's a lot you have to learn about Mururoa. We'll be going over on the first flight tomorrow morning so you only have today to get ready."

"Hold on." Brennan was surprised. "You're coming to the atoll with me?"

"Yes. I have a job there."

"What as?"

"A cleaner. It gets me into the cafeteria, the offices and some of the conference rooms." She paused. "Didn't my father tell you?"

"No." Brennan decided to make one last try. "Look," he said. "Believe whatever you like about me, but how about easing off a bit?"

"Do you want to start again, Mr. Brennan?" Martine Tumahai slipped the envelope back into her handbag, then placed her hands on her lap while she looked at him.

He detected what he thought might be a softening in her manner. "Where did you learn your English?" he said.

"In England. I was at school in France and at university in England. What else would you like to know about me?"

Brennan grinned. "Guess."

"What's a nice, well-educated Tahitian girl doing working as a cleaner on Mururoa atoll. Well, Mr. American drilling engineer, I'll tell you. Here in the islands my father is a very influential man but, after spending half his life working to save Tahiti from the French, the French are still here and a lot of Tahitian people are beginning to believe they'll always be here. We're already dependent on European money from the testing program and, unless someone does something very soon, in a few years there'll be nothing left of our culture. Along with my father and some other people I intend to make sure that doesn't happen."

"Is your mother Tahitian?" Brennan asked.

"My mother and younger sister were gang-raped by French construction workers in 1974, Mr. Brennan." Her hand unconsciously strayed to her necklace. "My sister is in an institution in Lyons, my mother is dead."

"Oh Jesus, I'm sorry." He wished he hadn't asked her.

"It's all right." Her voice was less brittle and she relaxed slightly. "I don't usually tell anyone."

"If your father's right, it won't just be people like you trying to get rid of the French," Brennan said. "Other countries are going to get involved real quick if there's really radioactive water in the sea around Mururoa."

"The French won't care. Tahiti is a long way from France."

"They don't own the goddamn Pacific," Brennan said.

"But they own this bit, don't they?" She smiled tightly. "I think we'd better get on with what we have to do. I need to know what size clothes you take, Mr. Brennan."

"My name's Zac," Brennan said.

"I know. What size are you?"

Brennan told her, watching while she scribbled in a notebook.

"I'll collect you here at six-thirty in the morning," she said. "I'll have two sets of clothes for you and some work boots and gloves." She glanced at him. "I'll bring your money, too."

He ignored the remark.

"You'll need these." She handed him a return airline ticket and plastic name tag. "The ticket is good for any of the shuttle flights between here and Mururoa over the next two weeks. You'll be working as a rigger's mate on the afternoon shift at a test site out in the lagoon. You'll be on one of the barges, I expect."

"Over the cavern they're going to concrete—right?"

She nodded. "They've driven lots of pipes into the floor of the lagoon and there's a big central tube that goes down a thousand meters into the cavern chimney. You'll see when you get there."

"Is the tube full of radioactive seawater?"

"Probably, otherwise they wouldn't be bothering to seal the cavern. You realize the water has to go somewhere, don't you? When the high-pressure concrete's pumped into the tube."

"Sure," Brennan said. "Back down into the cavern. Then into the atoll rock structure and out of the damn crack."

"Into the ocean, Mr. Brennan. The ocean the French use as their own private sewer. And in a few days when the level of radioactivity has died down, no one will know what they've done."

"How many tons of concrete will it take to plug the hole?" Brennan asked.

She raised her eyebrows. "I thought you'd work that out for us. We know how many kilotons were exploded there and we know the depth of the test so I can give you the size of the cavern, the quantity of rock inside it and the size of the chimney. Surely you can—"

"Okay, okay," he interrupted. "I just figured someone might've done the sums already. When do you think the French are going to start?"

"Judging by the equipment in the lagoon, the day after tomorrow—maybe the day after that. I've been here in Papeete for nearly two weeks so I'm not sure."

"But you've got other people over on the atoll, haven't you?" Brennan said.

"Yes, but only two of them know about you and it's not a good idea to phone anyone on Mururoa from Papeete because of the DGSE. They listen to a lot of the calls."

"Who are the DGSE?"

"Direction Générale de la Sécurité Extérieure." She slipped easily into French. "The French equivalent of your CIA."

"Are they any good?"

"Sometimes. They're the people who sank the first Rainbow Warrior in New Zealand to stop it coming to Mururoa. At one time everyone thought Greenpeace would keep on sending protest ships but . . ." Her voice trailed off. "The DGSE have their main office for French Polynesia in Tahiti and another special one on the atoll."

"What do they do?" Brennan rolled another cigarette.

"Watch, listen. Try and find out who the Tahitian activists are and look after security on the atoll." She smiled very slightly. "Lately they've been in a panic because Soviet submarines have started turning up to monitor the tests. Someone was supposed to have seen one. There was a huge fuss about it a couple of weeks ago in the local papers and in France, too."

Brennan wasn't surprised the Russians had arrived. If anything, the disintegration of the Warsaw Pact had made them more nervous of the West. The Soviet presence had been growing around Hawaii for some time, and in the last year Russian submarines had been showing up just about everywhere. He wondered if there were any here now.

"Maybe we could fix it so your French friends drop a nuke on a Soviet sub," he said.

Her smile had gone.

"Where are the transducers and the receiver?" he asked.

"Already on the atoll. I think there are thirty-five transducers altogether. My father said you should try to use them all."

Brennan did a quick calculation. "That's a reading about every hundred feet down," he said. "Pretty damn good if they all work okay."

"There's a camera for you, too, on the atoll, so you can photograph the core samples."

"Great." Brennan lit his cigarette. "John Carlisle's going to have a look at any pictures I take back."

"My father told me. He said Mr. Carlisle was very kind."

Her remark amused him. Ironically, by staying in Hawaii instead of flying here to work out on a barge and get ripped up by Tumahai's daughter, John had become the good guy. Although, Brennan thought, since she had started talking about the atoll instead of the money her responses had been less icy.

He studied her more closely, searching for some visible signs of a thaw.

Aware of his eyes, she touched her necklace again, then self-consciously adjusted the jacket of her suit.

"What else have you got to tell me?" Brennan said.

"If you have a piece of paper I'll sketch the layout of the atoll for you. To show you where the barracks are—and the mess halls and the laboratories." She hesitated. "There's one other thing, I suppose."

"About the atoll?" Brennan went to find some hotel writing paper.

"No." She shook her head. "Well, not really. You see, one of the girls in the overseas office gives me photocopies of some of the letters she types. Mostly they're routine communications to Paris but sometimes there's information in them that we can use."

"Like what? What kind of information?"

"We're not sure. Over the last few months there have been references to what the French are calling a fallback solution. That's not a proper translation but it's the best way of describing it in English. It's never more than just a few words but my father believes it could be important."

"But you don't know what it means?" Brennan said.

"No. Unless it's another way of filling or sealing off the caverns if the concreting doesn't work. I thought I'd tell you in case you come across some special kind of equipment when you're on the atoll—because you're an engineer."

"I'm going to have my hands pretty full with the core samples and the transducers," Brennan said. He laid a sheet of paper on the table in front of her. "I'll look, though."

"Thank you."

She wrote some figures at the top of the sheet. "This is the number of a safe-deposit box in the Bank of Tahiti. It's near the Bougainville post office. When you get back here from the atoll, put the results from the transducers in it with your report on the core samples. My father will have them collected as soon as you telephone him." She wrote down two more numbers. "This is my father's phone number in Papeete, the other one is for emergencies. Only use it if you get into trouble or if you need something quickly. Don't call my father."

"Whose number is it?"

"Just a friend on one of the other islands. It's a safe number." Smoothing down the paper, she began drawing a picture of the atoll.

He watched in silence, noticing for the first time the scratches and calluses on her hands.

When she had completed the outline of the island he leaned forward to examine a shaded area on which she had written the word *base.*

"Do most of the people live permanently on Mururoa?" Brennan asked.

"Now they do. Up until 1962 no one lived on the atoll at all. It was uninhabited. Right now the French have around thirty-five hundred people there."

"Christ." Brennan was astonished. "I had no idea."

"It's usually more like two thousand but people are pouring in from everywhere. All the flights are full. That's why it's been easy to make arrangements for you." She stopped drawing. "It's a big operation, Mr. Brennan. It costs over two million francs just to drill the hole for one underground test and another thirty-five million to carry out a test."

He pointed to a dot she had drawn in the lagoon. "Is that the cavern they're going to concrete?"

She nodded. "Yes. Louise. All the test sites have names. Most of them are along the reef here." She drew a series of dots along the northwest coast of the atoll.

"How deep's the water in the lagoon?" Brennan asked.

"I'm not sure. About fifty meters, I think. Why?"

"I need to know because of calculating the depth for each transducer."

"Oh, yes. Of course." She turned the paper over and began sketching again, identifying individual areas and buildings by name before moving to the next.

When she had finished, she put her pen away and gave

him the map. "I haven't drawn in all the roads," she said. "You only want an idea of where things are, don't you?"

"I guess," Brennan said. "Whereabouts are the core samples?"

"In this building here." She pointed. "It's a sort of combined warehouse and laboratory for the drilling technicians. Unless they have an especially urgent job, people only work there on day shift, so it won't be difficult for you to get in."

"Martine, have you seen these samples yourself?" He used her name deliberately.

"Yes." She appeared not to have noticed. "Not close up, though. They just look like cylinders of rock."

"Okay," Brennan said. "Thanks for the map. It gives me a pretty good idea of the layout. What about the transducers and the receiver and the camera?"

"One of our men has them. He'll be on your shift with you. Wait until he introduces himself before you do anything."

"How will I know he's the right guy?"

"He'll call you Brennan. You didn't look at your badge."

Brennan looked. It said ATKINS, R. J.

The same faint smile was on her lips. She stood up. "I'll be here at six thirty tomorrow, Mr. Atkins. That gives you plenty of time to get used to your new name."

"I'll work on it."

"Goodbye, then." She went to the door. "Try not to worry about your money, won't you?"

When she had gone, Brennan spent the best part of an hour lying on his bed studying the map. Then he went out to explore Papeete and find a bar.

From the air the atoll appeared to be deserted—a chain of white coral surrounding the flat green lagoon with no evidence of either buildings or people. The colors were almost too brilliant, Brennan thought, as though he were looking at a photograph of the island—or a painting in which the colors had been enhanced to disguise what was going on there.

The aircraft started its descent, banking slightly as the pilot adjusted his course for the run in.

"It always looks lovely like this, even in the winter."

The girl who spoke from the seat beside him was barely recognizable as the Martine Tumahai who had visited him yesterday. Gone were the smart clothes, the pearl necklace and the expensive handbag. In their place were jeans, a worn-out denim jacket and an excess of cheap jewelry. Her manner had changed too.

Brennan pointed out the window. "Is that the airstrip?"

She leaned across, apparently unconcerned when her breasts brushed against him. "Yes. You can see the roads as well now, and the wall along the reef." She slumped back into her seat. "Okay, Brennan, from here on we don't know each other."

Since her arrival at his hotel this morning, instead of addressing him as Mr. Brennan, she had been using his last name. To begin with, believing the change might have more to do with her change of clothes than any improvement in her attitude toward him, Brennan had been cautious. But, so far, apart from one or two awkward minutes when she'd given him the cash and another check, she seemed less aggressive and more willing to talk.

"Atkins," he said. "Remember?"

"You're the one who has to remember." She studied him briefly. "You know, you still look American."

Seeing as just about everyone on the aircraft was dressed in the same kind of clothes that Martine had insisted he wear this morning, Brennan had thought his disguise was pretty good. "Does it matter?"

She frowned. "I suppose not. There are Canadians, Englishmen and other Americans on the atoll."

"If we don't know each other, hadn't you better stop talking to me?" he said.

"I'm just a simple island vahine. People think you're trying to pick me up." She smiled sweetly. "Don't worry about it. I'll fix things after we've landed."

From the window now Brennan could see how wrong his first impression of the atoll had really been. Amid the palm trees was the mass of buildings Martine had drawn on her map. Dormitories, tennis courts, swimming pools, huge concrete-block houses and storage compounds were spread over an enormous area of the reef. Along the coastal strip, trailing clouds of dust, cars and trucks were traveling in both directions, while far out in the lagoon two drilling derricks were being serviced by a flotilla of boats and barges.

There was a glimpse of a modern harbor jammed with freighters and a number of larger ships before the aircraft touched down and began to taxi.

Martine unbuckled her seat belt. "Welcome to Mururoa," she said.

"It's about a hundred times bigger than I expected," Brennan said. Because of the scale of the installation he felt vaguely uneasy.

"I told you. People don't understand. This isn't a tiny Pacific island operation but, outside of France, hardly anyone realizes." She smiled. "There's one reason for that, though. Do you know what Mururoa means in Tahitian?"

Brennan shook his head.

"It means Great Secret."

"Hell of a secret," Brennan grunted. "I'm going to get lost around here if I'm not careful. Where can I find you if I need to talk?"

"You can't." She paused. "Well, not easily. Women all sleep in one dormitory and it's guarded all the time to stop any trouble. I'll try and meet you somewhere in a couple of days. One evening maybe."

"That won't do," Brennan said. "Trying isn't good enough. You're paying me a heap of money to get results from the transducers and for my opinion on these core samples. I can stick a report in your safe deposit box in Papeete but you'll get a whole lot more information by talking to me—finding out what I've seen and what I think's going on."

"All right. Talk to my father when you get back to Tahiti."

"It'd be a good idea, don't you think?" Brennan said.

"Yes, as long as you meet him somewhere safe. Don't use the telephone."

The aircraft had come to a halt outside a small white-washed terminal. Ground crews were already busy unloading mail and baggage. Inside the plane most passengers were on their feet, preparing to disembark.

"There's a building with a big radar dish on its roof," she said. "Go to the office on the ground floor where they process new arrivals. Just show them your name tag and say you were hired in Papeete. No one'll ask any questions."

"Should I speak English?" Brennan asked.

"You might as well. Then they'll explain where you have to go in English."

"Okay." He stood up, waiting for her to leave her seat. "This is your project," he said. "How about wishing me luck?"

"I think you're the kind of man who makes his own luck, Mr. Atkins."

Brennan was less confident. From what he'd seen already he thought there was a chance that Tumahai and his daughter might have seriously underestimated the job.

He followed her down the aisle and out onto the tarmac, where the heat hit him like a wall. Although it was still early in the morning the temperature and humidity were worse than anything he had experienced anywhere in Hawaii.

Martine was walking quickly away. He sprinted to catch

up with her. As he drew level, she swung around and stamped her foot. "*Cochon*," she shouted. "American pig." Then she spat on the ground and slapped him hard across the face.

With his cheek stinging from the blow, Brennan was trying not to laugh.

"Goodbye, Brennan," she whispered. "If I don't see you again, have a nice time with your money."

By the end of the afternoon shift on his first day, Brennan's unease had given way to apprehension. Working as a member of a team assigned to test site Louise in the lagoon, it had not been hard to sense that something was fundamentally wrong and, already, he had clear evidence that the French were trying to act too quickly in too many places.

According to scraps of conversation he had overheard, it had taken more than two weeks to install the pipework above the cavern. Preparations for pumping the concrete were well advanced, yet at six o'clock today all of the barges had been recalled to the reef and the entire fifty-man team dispatched in trucks to test site Giselle four kilometers away on the coast road.

There, to Brennan's considerable surprise, he had been confronted by an identical installation—another giant octopus of pipes, this one straddling the reef. Apart from being sited on coral rather than out in the water of the lagoon, the layout was the same—a large vertical steel tube connecting the cavern chimney to the outside world and, high above the ground near the top of the tube, a welded junction for the twelve smaller horizontal pipes that formed the arms of the octopus. These radiated outward for nearly a hundred feet before bending downward to penetrate shallow holes bored in the surface coral.

It was into this network of pipes that the concrete would be pumped, filling the gaps between rocks inside the cavern, filling the empty chimney and dispersing a layer of concrete through the coral immediately above the cavern.

Because the installation was so large and so distinctive, Brennan had started searching for others on the skyline. When he found them, his apprehension had set in.

The French were not making ready to seal off one cavern under the lagoon but, as far as he could tell, at least six others on dry land.

In most places, even at low tide, the reef was only a few feet above sea level and from his vantage point on the scaffolding above Giselle he had been able to pick out the men and drilling rigs at work on the other sites. All of them displayed the characteristic central tube, many already having some or all of the horizontal pipes in place.

The revelation had disturbed him, making him wonder if he had somehow misunderstood what he had seen. But that evening, when he came off his shift at ten o'clock, his fears had been confirmed. Brennan had eaten in one of the mess halls with two men from his team—Henri, a Frenchman from Marseilles, and a Tahitian supervisor called Tommy Taufa. Both men had been working on the atoll for over a year and both had told Brennan the CEP were busy with concreting programs at a number of different sites.

Now, sitting outside his bunkhouse smoking, Brennan's mind was grappling with too many unknowns. Either Tumahai and Martine had failed to properly comprehend what was going on, or they had deliberately lied to him. Or had everything happened so quickly that their intelligence system had failed to keep up with events?

Events, Brennan thought, that added up to one enormous headache for the CEP. The French didn't just have a problem with Louise—they had problems all over the damned atoll. A few days ago Louise was nearly ready to be plugged. Now Giselle had priority. Tomorrow another cavern somewhere else could start to flood.

Still with one cigarette in his mouth, Brennan began to roll another.

"Hey, Atkins." Taufa had come to find him. He was a stocky, muscular man with forearms bigger than Brennan's thighs.

"Hi." Brennan moved along on the bench to make room for him.

"You build that cigarette for me, *oui?*" Taufa's English was marginal but understandable.

Brennan gave it to him. "Is it always as hot as this at night?" he asked.

"Ah. You want cold, you go inside and sit by the air conditioner."

"I like it out here." Brennan handed him his lighter.

When the Tahitian returned it, something else was in his hand. Even in the dark Brennan knew what it was—a miniature, 16-millimeter Minolta camera.

He decided to be cautious. "What's this?" he said.

"You understand, I think, Monsieur Brennan."

"My name's Atkins."

"That is not what Mademoiselle Tumahai has told me." Taufa revealed a row of large white teeth. "You are the American Brennan. I am to help with the transducers and take you to the place where there are the borings from the rock."

"Core samples?" Brennan said.

"Yes." Taufa drew heavily on his cigarette. "You wish we go tonight?"

"I don't know." Brennan wanted more time to think.

"If the concrete is pumped at Giselle tomorrow we will work twelve hours on shift, maybe more. In the sun of the afternoon and after the hot night you will be no good for using the camera. It is better we go tonight."

Brennan was still uncertain. Everything was happening at once. He had no data on the size of the cavern for Giselle and without the couple of days' grace he'd been expecting in which to collect more information, he was already struggling.

"Can you take me to Miss Tumahai?" Brennan said.

"It is difficult. You have questions for her?"

"I can't put the transducers into the concrete unless someone tells me how big the cavern and chimney are. I have to do calculations."

"The Giselle cavern?"

"Yes."

Taufa withdrew a notebook from the pocket of his shorts. "Please, your cigarette lighter for me to see in the dark."

Brennan held the lighter while the Tahitian thumbed through pages of numbers.

"The test at Giselle was a little one," Taufa said. "Fifty kilotons at a depth of eight hundred meters. She was on May twelfth in 1984."

"That's no good," Brennan said. "The size of the explosion doesn't mean anything. I've got to have the cavern and chimney dimensions."

"Please. You will be patient." Taufa turned to a chart in the back of the notebook. "The Giselle cavern she is sixty-four meters in diameter with a chimney of one hundred and forty-eight meters upward into the atoll. For the hole which we make for the big tube I can tell you the cavern is filled to the very top with the loose rocks."

Before the Tahitian had finished speaking, Brennan knew he had misjudged him. Just as there were two Martine Tumahais, there were two Taufas—the good-natured, uncomplicated Polynesian who worked on the atoll and the other Taufa who worked for Martine and her father on a different level altogether.

"You're no more of a goddamn rigger than I am," Brennan said.

Taufa closed his notebook. "On the atoll I am drilling

supervisor," he said. "But I am also three quarters pure Tahitian."

Brennan smiled at him. "Miss Tumahai didn't give me your name," he said.

"Ah. She is a careful one. And very pretty, eh?" Taufa grinned widely. "Like a wild cat you want to touch except you know it will scratch your eyes out."

The analogy wasn't half bad, Brennan thought. A colorful and fair description of the lady. He held up the camera. "Okay. If you think tonight's a good time—let's go."

From the barracks it was a fifteen-minute walk to the laboratory, a long, single-story wooden building near the harbor. Most of the lights appeared to be switched on and the grounds outside were illuminated by floodlamps strung between palm trees. Brennan searched for signs of life but the building appeared to be empty.

"Are you sure no one's working in there?" he said.

"I am sure." Taufa pointed to a large oil storage tank. "We use the door which is in the shadow from that."

"It'll be locked, won't it?" Brennan held up a hand to shield his eyes from the glare.

Taufa took a key from his pocket. "I have keys to four CEP offices and for this building also. It is past eleven-thirty, yes?"

Brennan looked at his watch. "Yeah, just."

"Then we will not be disturbed. Here there are no guards or patrols after eleven o'clock at night. You understand this is a low-security area for the French. They believe no one is interested in their pieces of rock." Taufa led the way over to the tank. "I will go first to open the door, then you will come."

"All right." Brennan watched the Tahitian saunter across to the building, waiting for Taufa to unlock the door before he joined him.

"The rock drillings are in one room," Taufa said. "Please to follow me."

The room was not a room but an open storage bay taking up the full width of the building at the northeast end. When Martine had said the complex was half warehouse, Brennan hadn't expected anything quite this size.

In front of him, standing on the concrete floor, were row upon row of core samples, hundreds of them, each tagged with a colored plastic label.

"Christ," Brennan said. "Where the hell are all these from?" He answered his own question by kneeling down to inspect some of the labels.

"They are Louise or Giselle?" Taufa queried.

"Brigitte, Hortensia, Jasmin." Brennan crawled over to read some more. "Iris, Thérèse, Giselle, Paulette, Louise. They're from everywhere."

"Ah." Taufa looked embarrassed. "Before I have seen these only from the outside through the window. I had thought they were for one hole only but from many different depths in the rock."

Brennan had suddenly become too busy to answer. Instead of having to examine dozens of samples from one test site, the French had done the job for him. The labels told him precisely what he had come here to find out.

Each tag bore the name of the site, a date and the depth from which the sample had been obtained. But of more significance was the color of the labels. Green labels identified samples of limestone above the clay layer, red labels were used for samples of pure volcanic basalt from below the clay. And, to Brennan's satisfaction, labels exhibiting red and green stripes were attached to any sample taken from the clay-rich transition layer between the limestone and the basalt.

For the next few minutes he did nothing but inspect samples with striped labels, scrambling on his knees from one set to another.

Taufa observed in silence.

When Brennan finally stood up, his face was serious. "It's

about three hundred and twenty meters down from sea level over the whole atoll," he said. "The clay layer, I mean. Up to four hundred meters in some places. Every single sample in this place has been taken at a depth somewhere between three hundred and four hundred meters."

"From how many different sites?" Taufa asked.

"Twenty maybe. I didn't count."

"And the *couche d'argile*—the clay layer, she is okay?"

Very slowly Brennan shook his head. "She sure isn't. Look at this." He picked up one of the cylinders of rock. It was nearly two feet long, four inches in diameter and so heavy he had difficulty in holding it without shaking.

"You see those flecks and the dirty, mud-colored section near the top," he said.

"Oui."

"Well, that's what's left of your clay layer. It's supposed to be around thirty meters thick—ninety feet."

"Then there is no barrier to radioactive water if it is coming up through the fractured rock?" Taufa took the sample without effort and replaced it on the floor.

"Not at this site there isn't." Brennan read the label. "Jasmin. Not at any of these others either by the look of it."

"Then it is very bad," Taufa said. "We shall take photographs for Tumahai to give to the newspapers, yes?"

"Yes. If you can hold the samples, I'll shoot off the whole roll of film. Try and swing the tags around so I get them in the picture."

Brennan checked the camera, trying to concentrate on what he was doing instead of worrying about the atoll. Not even rudimentary analysis of the samples had been necessary. CEP geologists had already learned what Brennan was being paid to discover. That cracks in the atoll were allowing seawater into many caverns was bad enough. That the clay layer had been compressed to almost nothing by the explosions had turned a serious problem into a disaster of frightening proportions.

When the film was finished he put the Minolta in his pocket and asked Taufa if there was anything else to see.

"I do not know." The Tahitian's forehead was beaded in sweat from the strain of lifting so many samples.

"Let's have a quick look before we go."

Although the locks on the laboratory doors refused to cooperate with Taufa's key, and other rooms were either empty or contained equipment of no interest. Brennan did come across something interesting in another part of the warehouse: wooden boxes containing pumps—high-capacity concreting pumps of the kind he had seen at Louise and Giselle today. He counted over seventy of them.

"We go now?" Taufa said.

Brennan nodded. He followed the Tahitian back to the barracks, preoccupied with what he had learned and wondering what more he might discover once the transducers began sending their signals from the broken heart of Mururoa.

High on the pipework above the reef the sun was the enemy. Without leather gloves, wrenches were too hot to hold and Brennan was being continuously blinded by the sweat pouring into his eyes. Steadying himself against the catwalk rail he removed his hard hat, letting the breeze blow through his hair while he looked down.

Below on the reef, the big diesels were already thumping, driving the concrete pumps and the conveyor belts that fed them. All around him, armored hoses carrying high-pressure concrete to the octopus were pulsing in unison as though they were alive, shaking the scaffolding and the catwalk on which he stood.

Along the coast road the convoy of trucks bringing concrete to Giselle was now nearly a quarter of a mile long. Through the clouds of coral dust Brennan could see empty trucks already returning to the base for another load. It was time for him to begin.

He started his climb back to the ground, hoping Taufa would be ready.

The night before, after he had hidden the camera in his locker, Brennan had spent several hours calculating how many tons of concrete would be needed. The figure was staggering. Even though the cavern itself was supposed to be jammed with rock, if it was to be properly sealed, concrete would have to be forced into the gaps between the rubble before the chimney could be filled. And to do this, Brennan had calculated, Giselle would require more than three thousand tons of concrete in all—a hundred and fifty truckloads.

Today, during the drive out to the site, he had seen evidence of how large the operations at the atoll would eventually become. Ships from Australia, New Zealand and North America were discharging ballast and cement at the harbor at an unbelievable rate. Giselle, Louise and the other sites under preparation were only the beginning of what the French were trying to do—the tip of an iceberg so large and so dangerous that Brennan could not imagine how much it would cost to control it.

Taufa was waiting for him by one of the concrete hoppers. "A hot bastard today like I tell you, eh?" He grinned.

"You said it." Brennan spat out a mouthful of dust. "Have you got the transducers?"

"Over there." Taufa pointed. "In the box."

"Okay." Brennan glanced at his notes then checked his watch. "I reckon the first one goes in around two thirty. That's pretty soon."

"And the last one?" Taufa asked.

"At the rate we're pumping, about ten o'clock tonight. We're on shift right through until it's finished so we should be okay."

"Unless there is a problem. Two of the pumps are blocked already."

"Reciprocating pumps block all the time," Brennan said. "It's usually easy enough to get them going again."

"We throw the transducers into the concrete on the belt conveyors, yes?"

Brennan nodded. "And hope like hell they don't get chewed up on their way through the pump valves."

"I will do it," Taufa said. "But you must tell me the time for each one."

"Right. Let's go and get them."

Packed in individual compartments inside the box, the transducers were gleaming white spheres about the size of a large marble, each engraved with a signal frequency and the depth from which it would transmit.

Being careful not to touch the tiny protruding pin that was the switch to turn it on, Brennan took one from the box. For its size it was remarkably heavy. "I hope these babies work," he said. "They're going on a hell of a ride."

"They will slide between the rocks in the cavern, you think?" Taufa asked.

"Some of them will." Brennan found one with eight hundred meters written on it. He depressed the pin until it clicked in flush with the surface. "Here." He tossed it to Taufa. "That's the first. It's transmitting right now."

"There are some marked with twelve hundred meters. I have seen them."

"Yeah, I know. But they were for Louise. You said Giselle's only eight hundred meters deep."

"Ah." The big Tahitian looked awkward. "We shall have some left over. I have not been thinking again."

Brennan grinned at him. "Tommy, my friend, there's nothing much wrong with your thinking." He looked at his watch again. "You'd better get going. Make sure no one sees what you're doing."

Taufa folded his hand round the transducer. "The

French are too stupid to be watching but I will be careful." He paused. "This morning you have seen the bulletins about swimming which have been put up?"

"Yes." Brennan had read them along with everyone else.

"So no one is permitted now to swim in the lagoon and also outside the reef between the test sites at Grue and Aline where the lagoon is open to the sea. You will tell me please if you think the radioactivity has become more bad in the water."

"What do you think?"

"I think the atoll she is sick." Taufa turned to leave. "Maybe what we do here today will fix it, eh?"

Brennan rolled a cigarette, watching Taufa walk away into the dust and noise. If what he'd learned so far was any indication, the atoll wasn't just sick, it was dying—hemorrhaging infected water out into the ocean. When Tumahai had asked Carlisle to help him, he hadn't known the half of it.

Two uniformed CEP supervisors were approaching Brennan. He stuck the cigarette in his mouth, nodded pleasantly at them, then put on his gloves and climbed back onto the octopus.

For the next seven and a half hours activity at the site was continuous as three thousand tons of liquid concrete were injected into the fabric of the atoll, penetrating the cavern, the rocks and the coral. Only when the last truck had gone and the pumps had stopped for the last time did silence finally fall over the reef at Giselle.

Weary men were switching off the rows of floodlights or closing valves, thankful that the job was over and that nothing had gone wrong.

For as far as Brennan could see, the ground was covered in dust. Illuminated in the moonlight, hoppers, generators, pumps and conveyors all reflected the same white glow while, in the sky above him, steel pipes full of solidifying concrete shone like some unearthly monument to commemorate the sealing of the cavern deep below it.

For Brennan, the events of the last two days needed no commemoration. His examination of the core samples and everything else he'd seen were a guarantee that he would never forget what was happening here—the beginning of a containment program so huge that even a country the size of France would be hard pressed to complete it.

"So, she is done." Taufa interrupted his thoughts.

"This one," Brennan said. "Only this one."

"We take the readings now?"

"Did you bring the receiver?" For some reason Brennan hadn't thought of trying to get a scan tonight.

"It is hidden. I have put it over by the fuel tanker." Taufa's teeth gleamed in the moonlight. "We wait now here in the dark until everyone has gone home to the base. Then we take the readings."

"And how do we get back to the base?" Brennan inquired.

Taufa laughed. "We walk. If you are too tired, I carry you, eh?"

Tired as he was, Brennan knew there were advantages in doing the job straight away. He was not sure whether some transducers might be crushed as the concrete solidified but this way they would avoid the risk altogether and, even though Tumahai had said the lithium batteries in the transducers were good for three days, the signals would never be stronger than they were at the moment.

"Okay," he said. "We'd better lose ourselves somewhere while those guys get their ride back."

"You come to where I put the receiver." The Tahitian headed off into the shadows.

The receiver was the size of a small suitcase. It consisted of two encapsulated electronic modules, a high-speed chart recorder and a telescopic aerial.

Brennan shared a cigarette with Taufa while they waited

for the last personnel carrier to disappear. Now on the reef there was only the sound of surf against the wall outside the coral and an occasional creak from cooling pipework.

"Damn." Brennan had suddenly thought of something. "How many transducers did we use?"

"Twenty-six. There are nine still in the box. There is a problem?"

"Yeah, I think so. Did you switch the whole lot on?"

Taufa nodded. "So I would not forget any."

"That means those little bastards in the box are transmitting, too," Brennan said. "We'll have to find out what depths they were for so we can wipe their signals off the chart."

"I am sorry." Taufa stubbed out the cigarette. "It is my mistake. But we can start to make the recording. It is one button here on the receiver to push."

"Okay. I'll go and get them." Brennan wandered off. Already his legs were stiffening from the unaccustomed exercise. A day on Mururoa crawling around on a bunch of scaffolding was not the same as a day on the Big Island drilling holes for John Carlisle, he thought, even if the money was a lot, lot better. He wondered what Carlisle would say when he heard the news about the atoll.

Picking up the nearly empty box of transducers he turned around. As he did so, two hundred feet away where Taufa was crouched over the receiver, the night exploded.

For an instant, in the tremendous flash, he saw the Tahitian's broken body flung against the tanker. Then the shock wave hit him.

FOUR

STUNNED by the blast, barely conscious and jammed hard against the scaffolding face down in the dust, Brennan could neither hear nor see.

Slowly pain brought back his senses. He rolled onto his side, trying to discover what was wrong with his leg. Both his eyes were filled with grit and he was choking. Using a finger to clear the dust from his mouth, he rubbed saliva into his eyes so he could see. Not far away, with its rear axle enveloped in flame, the upturned tanker stood in a pool of burning fuel.

Sitting up he gingerly explored his right leg, searching for the source of the pain. Just below his knee in the fleshy part of his calf, Brennan found it—a sliver of metal protruding from his jeans. Even brushing his fingers against it made him break out in a sweat.

The flames were higher around the tanker now and in the distance sirens had started wailing.

Brennan scrambled to his feet, testing his leg against the ground to see if it would bear his weight. Although it would be five minutes before the first vehicles reached the site, the tanker could blow at any second.

Behind him lay the lagoon; ahead, the reef wall and the open sea.

He chose the wall.

With each step his jeans tugged at the splinter. Clenching his teeth he grabbed hold of it and pulled. It came out easily—a pointed fragment of steel nearly an inch and a half long. He threw it away and limped over to the wall. The pain was more bearable but he could feel blood running down his calf. Now he could see the lights of trucks speeding toward him along the coast road.

Brennan eased himself over the wall, sliding feet first onto the sloping coral shelf. Waves lapped over his boots as he began to move away from the burning tanker.

After traveling what he thought was a safe distance he stopped to rest and sluice some handfuls of water over his face.

The trucks had not quite reached him when he heard the second explosion at the site.

Cautiously raising his head, he looked back. The whole octopus was illuminated by an orange glow—one arm emerging from a billowing ball of fire where the tanker had been.

He continued watching while the trucks swept by, heading for Giselle with their headlights cutting through the smoke. The flames were dying quickly, either, he thought, because the tanker had been all but empty or because there was nothing else on the reef to burn.

Soon men would discover Taufa's body and begin the search for what had caused the blast. And then another search would start—for more bodies or for other men who might be missing from the base.

Only by accident had Brennan survived the explosion—an explosion that he was certain had been meant for him. Whoever wired the charge into the receiver hadn't been gunning for Taufa, they'd been after the foreigner on the atoll—a foreigner they still had every chance of finding.

He rolled up his jeans, allowing the seawater to wash over the wound in his leg. Then Brennan started out on his long and painful walk back to base.

It was ten minutes before midnight when he eventually reached the palms that flanked the runway. Here, because there was no foreshore, the reef wall was much higher on the seaward side. Waist-deep in water, stumbling and sliding over coral rocks the size of cars, he was close to exhaustion.

Four kilometers behind him at Giselle, lights still flickered over the octopus, but traffic on the coast road had died down some time ago and he guessed most of the trucks and fire engines would have already returned here to the base.

With some difficulty Brennan hauled himself up to peer over the wall. The compound was ablaze with lights and everyone appeared to be out of bed. Groups of men stood outside their barracks talking, most of them only half dressed. Others who had obviously returned from the site were sitting around recounting what they had seen there to their fellow workers.

Brennan had two priorities. Retrieve the camera from his locker, then, before the hunt for him began in earnest, find some way of getting off the atoll.

Wincing from the pain in his calf, he climbed over the wall and walked very slowly across the runway, making for the shadows behind the mess hall. Now that he was out of the water he could feel the blood soaking into his sock and his jeans.

Gathered in the doorway of his dormitory, half a dozen men were laughing at something—men who might either notice the blood or wonder how he had managed to get so wet. He waited for them to disperse, not sure whether he should go to his locker. Beneath his shirt in his body belt was Brennan's insurance—the money from Martine. With it, if he avoided the risk of trying to collect the camera and if his luck held, there was a slim chance that he could buy his way onto one of the freighters in the harbor. Or was he exaggerating the risk? Were the French still searching for him somewhere at Giselle?

Brennan decided.

Entering the building behind two other men he turned left into a passageway and headed for the locker room. Halfway down the corridor he stopped. Ahead of him the steel door of his locker lay broken on the floor. It was severely bent and he could see the scratches where someone had used a crowbar or an ax to smash the hinges.

At the end of the room two CEP officers stood talking to some of the riggers. Carefully Brennan retreated. His mouth was dry and he could feel his heart beating faster.

Once outside the barracks again he tried to think what he should do. Attempting to reach the harbor would be too dangerous now, he realized. If the French even suspected he was still alive, the harbor would be one of the first places they'd expect him to head for. He needed more time and somewhere to rest while he figured out a better way to escape from the atoll.

A hand touched his shoulder.

He swung around, fists clenched ready.

It was Martine. She was dressed in overalls with her hair tucked inside a baseball cap.

"Get out of the light," she whispered. "Over there by the latrines."

Trying not to limp, Brennan did as she said.

He leaned against the building, waiting for her to join him.

"For God's sake what's gone wrong?" she asked.

He told her.

"Taufa's dead?"

Brennan nodded. "It was pretty quick." He paused. "I'm sorry."

"They were after you." She moved so that her shadow fell

across his face. "I'm sure they didn't know about Tommy."

"They've got the camera too—from my locker. I photographed the samples last night."

"There's a rumor that someone was killed at Giselle tonight," she said. "I thought it was you. I came to ask Tommy what happened." She saw him grimace. "Oh my God, you're hurt. What is it?"

"I took a piece of steel in my leg. It's okay, I've pulled it out."

She gripped his arm. "Listen, you have to get away. The French are going to turn this place upside down looking for you."

"Do you think I don't know that?" Brennan said angrily. "The bastards must have been watching me ever since I got here. Somewhere along the way one of your so-called friends has started working for the other side. And whoever it is hasn't just screwed things for you and me—they killed Taufa."

She ignored his outburst. "Have you still got your airline ticket back to Tahiti?"

"What use is a goddamn airline ticket? The French'll be watching every plane out of here."

"Just tell me if you've got it."

"Yes. In my belt."

"And how bad is your leg?"

"All right." He changed his mind. "I'm not sure. It kind of hurts."

She thought for a moment. "Do you know where the cold store is? Where the meat and frozen vegetables are kept."

"Yes, I think so. It's all concrete and no windows, near the terminal. Is that it?"

She nodded. "At one end there's a tiny door facing the radio building. It leads to a crawl space under the floor. Go there now and wait for me. I'll be there in ten minutes."

"Hiding out underneath a cold store is just going to use

up time," Brennan said. "If you want to do something find a way for me to get on board one of those ships. Find a captain who's interested in money."

"Don't you trust me?" Martine said.

"Yes," he grunted. "Sure."

"Then go to the store, Brennan." She met his eyes. "Now, before all these people start going back to bed."

The more he considered his options the more apparent it was that he didn't have any. Without her help, no matter where he went or what he did, he was trapped on the atoll and sooner or later the CEP or the DGSE were going to run him down.

"Ten minutes," he said. "Right?"

"I promise."

He left her, keeping in the shadows of buildings, being careful to avoid men wearing CEP uniforms whenever he saw them. At the cold store he spent several minutes trying to find the door, finally locating it behind a pile of discarded cardboard boxes.

The crawl space was high enough for him to sit up providing he kept his neck bent, but the uneven ground beneath the floor made sitting more uncomfortable than lying down.

Sweating from his exertions he searched for an area where there was more room for him to move.

A flashlight beam announced Martine's arrival at the door.

"Brennan," she whispered. "Are you there? Where are you?"

"Over here."

She crawled over to him. "Let me see your leg," she instructed.

He rolled up the leg of his jeans while she held the flashlight.

"How does it look?" he asked.

"Deep. Keep still now. This is going to hurt."

He gasped. "Jesus Christ, what the hell are you doing?"

"Penicillin. I've injected a whole capsule right down inside." She wiped the blood away then covered the wound with an adhesive dressing. "Are you okay?"

Brennan didn't answer. He wondered if she was enjoying this.

"I brought you something," she said. Resting her flashlight in her lap she put a cigarette in his mouth and lit it for him.

As she leaned forward, Brennan saw the knife. It hung inside her overalls on a cord around her neck, an unsheathed steel blade with a braided leather handle.

"I have to go more or less straight away," she said. "I'll leave you the cigarettes and matches and you can have this too. I stole it from the sick bay." She handed him a small hypodermic syringe. "Only use it if you really have to—just a little at a time—not all of it."

"Morphine?" he said.

"Yes."

"I don't need morphine."

"You might. You have to last all night and behave normally on the plane in the morning."

"I've told you," Brennan said. "Forget about damn planes. The French'll stop me before I get anywhere near one."

"Not if they think you're dead, they won't. Not if they've already found your body." She took hold of his wrist. "Let me have your watch."

He pulled his arm away, suddenly understanding. "And you're going to provide them with a body?"

"Have you a better idea?" Her words were clipped. "I'll drop it off in the lagoon somewhere so it'll look as though you managed to crawl away after the explosion. All I have to do is make sure someone finds it before morning."

Brennan searched unsuccessfully for words. She had made the statement casually as if what she was proposing to do was unimportant. That she could seriously be considering murder was almost inconceivable. "What's the matter, Brennan?" She grasped his wrist again. "Would you rather stay here in this rathole until they find you?"

"Martine," he said gently. "This isn't the way." He could feel her hand trembling.

"Give me your watch and your name tag."

He passed them to her.

"I need to know how bad the fire was," she said. "Your face could've been burned, couldn't it?"

He nodded silently, still uncertain of his feelings but aware now that she was nothing like as calm as she would have him believe.

"All right, then. I'll bring clean clothes and another name tag for you in the morning. Stay here until I come back."

"Look." He stopped, not knowing what to say to her.

She sensed his confusion. "You saw Taufa die tonight, didn't you?"

"Yes."

"Well, that's how it is here, Brennan. It took the French a lot longer to kill my mother than it did for them to murder Tommy Taufa but they still killed them. They're dead, like hundreds of other Tahitians. You don't understand. It's been this way for the last twenty-nine years."

"I have a fair idea of what's going on here right now," he said. "I think I know what's happening."

"Tell me afterwards. I have to leave."

"You don't have to do this for me," he said quietly. "What about this other guy you've got on the atoll? Or I'll do it myself and take my chances. I'm not going to let you kill someone."

"You don't have any chances. You'd be dead before morning." She paused. "I can't ask anyone else—anyway, I'm not doing it for you."

"I'll come with you, then," he said.

"Don't be stupid. They're looking everywhere for you. The DSGE are out there." She began slithering over toward the door.

"Hey," Brennan whispered.

She hesitated. "What?"

He knew there wasn't any other way. It was either this or hand himself over to the French authorities. And, if the French did get hold of him, it would be too damned easy for them to find the real body of Zac Brennan at Giselle.

"Nothing," he said. "Be careful."

She turned her head. "Is that a way of offering me some of your luck?"

"You can have it all."

"Thanks." She continued crawling, then shone the flashlight briefly on his face before she disappeared.

Lying on his back on the coral beneath the building, Brennan struggled to control his imagination. He was back at the test site watching the girl use her knife—seeing her burn the face of a stranger—watching while she clipped his own watch and name tag onto the body.

Exhaustion combined with the throbbing in his leg was draining what little of his strength remained and making the nightmare worse—a nightmare in which the geological failure of the atoll was but a beginning. Again, in slow motion, he saw Taufa's body smash against the tanker and, this time, saw himself observing high above the octopus.

Drenched in sweat, Brennan sat up. Then he rolled back his sleeve and used the syringe.

Sunlight filtering through gaps in the base of the cold store told him it was morning. He struggled to wake up, searching for his missing watch to see what time it was.

Beside him, still asleep, Martine was curled up like a child, her hair spilling out from beneath her cap. In the open palm of her right hand lay the knife and near her wrist the sleeve of her jacket was badly charred.

This was another Martine Tumahai, Brennan thought. Not a child, not the well-dressed, well-bred young woman he had first met at his hotel, nor the innocent, doe-eyed vahine who worked as a cleaner on the atoll. This was Taufa's wild cat—a Tahitian guerrilla fighter still trying to hold the knife he was certain she had used last night.

He shook her gently by the shoulder.

At once her body stiffened, her fingers curling around the handle of the knife. She sat up quickly, banging her head on one of the floor joists.

"Easy," Brennan whispered. "It's me."

She rubbed her forehead. "What time is it?"

"I don't know."

"It's early, otherwise there'd be more noise outside." She blinked in a ray of sunlight. "How's your leg?"

"Better. Pretty stiff but it doesn't hurt so much." He wanted to ask her what had happened while he'd been asleep.

"You ought to have antibiotic pills."

"I'll have a cigarette instead," Brennan said. "I've got two left. What do you think?"

She shook her head, freeing the rest of her hair from the cap. "Someone might see the smoke, or smell it. There won't be any breeze yet."

"So what's the plan?"

"You catch the first plane. It's at ten past seven." She reached for a plastic bag she had been using as a pillow. "I've brought jeans and a clean shirt for you."

"And a new name tag?" Brennan said quietly.

She nodded. "Last night I didn't ask if you have your passport with you."

"I didn't think it'd be too smart to leave it lying around in the barracks." He patted the belt under his shirt. "It's in here."

"Right. Now, when you get to the terminal in Papeete, go straight to the UTA international desk. I phoned to make a reservation last night. You're wait-listed first class to Honolulu on flight 425 at ten fifteen this morning. That doesn't give you much time to check in so don't hang around."

"What about leaving here?" Brennan said. "You don't think there'll be a problem—me getting on the shuttle, I mean?"

"No. Not unless the DGSE listened to my phone call and have got suspicious. The French have found two bodies at Giselle. One of them is Taufa's and they think the other one is yours." From the way she spoke it was clear that she had no intention of explaining further.

Brennan said nothing.

She produced a banana from the pocket of her overalls. "Breakfast," she said. "I'm sorry I couldn't bring anything else."

"What about you?" He was hungry enough to eat a dozen bananas.

"You have it—while you tell me about the core samples and what the CEP have done about Giselle."

"It's not just Giselle," he said.

"I know. I've seen the pipes they've started installing at the other sites."

Speaking between mouthfuls of banana, Brennan outlined his fears about the atoll and described what he had concluded from examining the core samples.

When he had finished, her face was serious. "I'd better see if I can leave today or tomorrow," she said. "I'll have to tell my father."

"There's not a hell of a lot to tell him, is there? The French could be plugging the caverns as a precaution. If someone hadn't booby-trapped the receiver we'd have the information from the transducers and know for sure whether they're leaking or not. Instead of that we've got nothing." He reached inside his belt for the envelope. "Here, I don't want your money. I didn't do anything."

She took the check but left him holding a handful of notes. "You'd better keep the cash," she said awkwardly. "In case you need it."

Brennan stuffed the francs back in his belt. "What a mess," he said. "Taufa's dead and we haven't got a single piece of evidence your father can give the newspapers. The whole thing's been a waste of time and the goddamn French have got my film of the core samples. We can't even prove someone wired up the receiver with explosives."

"Perhaps the papers will listen anyway," she said.

"Why should they? Everyone already knows underground nuclear testing isn't exactly an environmentally clean pastime. Unless your father has hard proof, everyone'll figure he's just making waves again." Brennan thought for a minute. "I suppose you could try and get photos of the pipework at all the different sites. It might start people wondering what's going on."

"The CEP have armed guards on the sites," she said. "As of last night. I saw them at Giselle before I came back here."

He saw her hands were shaking. "Are you okay?" he asked.

"Yes." She smiled tightly. "Are you feeling protective or something?"

He smiled at her. "Look, you don't have to go on proving anything to me. Not now. I'm on your side, remember?"

"It's all gone so horribly wrong." She lay back on the coral with her hands behind her head. "I don't know what to do."

"As soon as I'm home I'll talk to John Carlisle. He's a pretty smart guy. He might have an idea."

"I don't think there's very much time." She turned onto her side to look at him. "They've stopped anyone swimming in the lagoon. This thing could be really bad, couldn't it?"

"Yeah. I figure there's a chance the caverns are leaking faster than the French can seal them off."

"What happens if you're right?"

Brennan shrugged. "The CEP will have to get some help, I guess. Without some sort of international collaboration to supply materials and the right equipment I don't think there's any way they'll be able to do the job by themselves. It'll be a massive operation to seal the atoll properly."

Martine sat up again. "The French won't ask for help. They'd never admit they made a mistake."

Outside men were talking. Brennan put a finger on his lips, not speaking again until the voices had faded away.

"Let me see Carlisle," he said. "I'll phone your father from Hawaii if we can think of something."

"No." She shook her head. "Use that other number I gave you. It's a house on Rangiroa. If my father and I aren't there leave a message so one of us can call you back."

"Okay." Taking the shirt and jeans from the plastic bag, Brennan began to change, struggling to keep the clothes as free of coral dust as he could. Both his sock and the dressing on his leg were saturated in dried blood but, as far as he could tell, there was no fresh bleeding and no signs of infection around the wound.

"I'll leave before you," she said, "so I can check on the time and make sure everything looks all right. You stay here until I come and kick on the door. That'll mean you have five minutes to get over to the air terminal." She reached out to pin the new identification tag onto his shirt.

Brennan tried to read the name. "Who am I this time?" he asked.

"Monsieur Drollet."

A very dead Monsieur Drollet, Brennan thought. A Frenchman who had died because Taufa had died, a French life for the life of the Tahitian supervisor—an eye for an eye in a struggle to prevent a tiny atoll from contaminating half of the South Pacific. Despite what Martine believed, gradually he was beginning to appreciate what was at stake, understanding why Martine Tumahai and people like her were prepared to do almost anything to stop the testing program. But were their efforts too late? And if they were, and if the French were really in big trouble, what the hell would the CEP do about it?

"Hey, Brennan." She interrupted his thoughts.

"What?"

"Goodbye."

He smiled at her again. "So long. I'll phone you anyway—after I've seen John. I'm sorry how things turned out."

To his surprise she leaned forward and kissed him quickly on the cheek. "I wasn't going to tell you this," she said. "But you're not such a bastard as I thought."

"Don't bank on it," he said. "But thanks."

"There's one thing you'd better do when you get to Papeete, Brennan. Before you get on the plane."

He lifted his boots. "Buy some shoes instead of these?"

"No. Get some deodorant." She tucked her hair inside the cap, then without either speaking again or once looking back, she crawled away and slipped quietly out of the door.

Through the slits in the boards, Brennan watched her go. More people were moving around outside now and somewhere nearby there was the sound of a truck being started. He hoped she had not misjudged the time.

Her kick on the door came unexpectedly, making him jump. It was barely ten minutes since she'd left the cold store.

Giving her a few seconds to walk away, Brennan eased the door open. The cardboard boxes were still there. Using them as a screen he scrambled out, squinting in the sunlight. The morning was windless and already very hot. Immediately ahead of him laborers were climbing into an open-backed personnel carrier.

Brennan cursed his luck. From where the truck was parked, ten or fifteen men had a clear view of the boxes and, unless it moved off very soon, the five minutes he had to board the shuttle were not going to be enough. It would take him at least two minutes to reach the terminal and, even if he could run on his leg, running was a sure way to attract attention.

He took a risk and stood up. At the same time the personnel carrier started to draw away.

Walking slowly, smoking one of his last two cigarettes, Brennan followed the narrow concrete path that skirted the end of the runway, increasing his pace only slightly as he approached the terminal.

Inside no one looked at him. He handed his ticket to the man at the check-in counter, aware of how fast his heart was beating from the throbbing in his leg. For the return flight to Papeete there was no official boarding pass, just a rubber stamp on his ticket stub.

"Baggage?" the man inquired.

Brennan shook his head. He took back his ticket, threw away his cigarette and hurried to join a stream of passengers already on their way across the tarmac.

Seconds later he was on board, seated in the rear of the aircraft, his head buried in a newspaper.

Not until the plane had taken off did he even start to relax. Although his leg was less painful, now that he was sitting down again, it was a reminder for him to stay alert. This was still French Polynesia and Papeete was no farther away from Mururoa than a phone call. Too anxious to allow himself to fall asleep, for much of the journey Brennan either dozed or pretended to read the paper.

At Papeete after an uneventful flight, he disembarked and reported directly to the girl at the UTA counter.

She checked his passport and returned it. "You're lucky

with your reservation," she said. "Economy's full right up and we only had two cancellations in first class."

"Can I get a razor somewhere?" Brennan was conscious of his appearance.

"There are razors in all the toilets on the plane, Mr. Brennan." She smiled. "You look as though you could use some sleep, too. Have a nice trip home."

In an attempt to freshen up, before take-off he washed, shaved, combed his hair and, in accordance with Martine's instructions, applied liberal quantities of airline after-shave and deodorant.

Back at his seat he found a glass of scotch and the cigarettes he'd asked for already on his armrest table.

Flight attendants closed the hatches, engines whined and all around him in the cabin there were clicks of seat belts being fastened.

Taking off into a cloudless sky, the DC-10 climbed steadily until the islands of French Polynesia became the innocent, unspoiled scraps of land he had once imagined them to be.

His forehead pressed against the window, Brennan watched them slowly melt away to nothing.

FIVE

FOR the second time in two days Stephanie stood naked in front of the bathroom mirror. What she saw was what she had seen yesterday—a reflection of herself too familiar to analyze. Yet, for her age, her figure was holding up well, she decided. Her stomach was flat, or flat enough, and she still had good legs. John had even said she had nice legs.

She abandoned her inspection, almost wishing she had found a flaw—some defect she could pretend was unattractive, something she knew he didn't like. Except that I don't know what he finds unattractive, Stephanie thought. Any more than I know any other damn thing about him.

Wrapping her housecoat round her she tiptoed to the kitchen and started making coffee. Because it was Sunday the traffic outside was quieter than it had been on the other mornings she'd spent at his apartment. Instead of the noise from cars and buses slowing for the intersection at the end of the road, she could hear a dog barking and, in the distance, the sound of a lawn mower at work.

She rummaged in a kitchen drawer for a pen, then poured herself some coffee and went back to the bedroom.

Carlisle was still asleep. He lay in the center of the bed with his back to her, half covered by a crumpled sheet.

She sat down beside him, balancing her cup on her knee, wondering why it was so important for her to understand how she felt about him. It was less than a week since they had first made love, yet already she sensed he was somehow tiring of her. Perhaps because her seduction of Carlisle had been more imagined than real, she thought. Perhaps he had been waiting and she had spoiled things by making it too easy. Either that or she was being introspective, searching for explanations when there was nothing to explain—when there was nothing really wrong.

She drew her finger down his spine to wake him up.

Carlisle turned over but kept his eyes closed. "You've brought me coffee," he said. "I can smell it."

"No, I haven't. This is mine." Stephanie made certain her cup was out of reach. "I'll get you some if you promise not to go back to sleep."

He studied her face. "It's Sunday," he said. "We don't have to go to work."

"So?"

"So put down your cup."

She shook her head.

Carlisle slipped a hand inside her housecoat.

"Stop it." She wriggled away, laughing, spilling coffee onto the bed.

He blotted it up with the sheet. "I told you to put it down."

"I'm here on business," she said primly. "I may be improperly dressed for a business meeting but we have things to discuss."

"What things?"

"Us. What we talked about last night. You know, about working in the same office at the university and then coming back here to sleep together."

He propped himself up on an elbow. "As long as the university doesn't find out, who cares?"

"That's pathetically transparent. You're only saying you

don't care because you want me to come back to bed, don't you?"

Carlisle grinned at her. "What did we decide last night?"

"This will remind you." She picked up an envelope from the bedside table, addressing it with the felt-tipped pen before she gave it to him.

Carlisle opened the envelope, reading the letter inside without changing his expression.

"Are you serious?" he said.

"Mm." She nodded. "That's my official resignation. It fixes things so I can move in here." She hesitated. "Properly, I mean. I'll either get another job or do something part time. What do you think?"

This time Carlisle grabbed her wrists, pulling her down on top of him. She pretended to struggle then allowed him to roll her over onto her back. Sitting on her legs, still holding her wrists, he looked down at her.

"If you move in with me I'll destroy whatever's left of your feminist ideals," he said.

"Okay. If that's what you want to do. You can let me go."

"I don't believe you." He released her cautiously.

His further intentions were interrupted by the phone.

"Leave it," she said. "The answering machine's on. We can call back later."

Brennan's voice came over the speaker.

"It's Zac." Carlisle jumped off the bed and sprinted into the living room.

Brennan was recording a message of four-letter words when Carlisle lifted the receiver.

"Sorry," Carlisle said, "it's me. Where are you?"

"Home. Why the hell don't you answer your phone if you're in your apartment?"

"I am answering it. I wasn't expecting you back so soon. How did it go?"

"Don't ask," Brennan grunted.

"Did you get the photos and a scan from the transducers?"

"You'd better come over," Brennan said. "I need to talk to you."

"It's Sunday. You come here. I'll buy you lunch."

"John, you don't understand. The whole thing went wrong. I've just got back from the hospital." Brennan sounded tense. "I'm not in the best shape to go anywhere right now."

Carlisle sat down. "What's the matter?"

"Not on the phone. I'll tell you when I see you. Just get on a plane."

Although the urgency in Zac's voice was unmistakable, Carlisle was reluctant to spoil his Sunday.

Stephanie had come to the phone. "Where is he?" she asked.

"Maui. He's home." Carlisle covered the mouthpiece with his hand. "He wants me to fly over. I'll tell him I'll go tomorrow."

"No." She shook her head. "Go today. We can both go."

"Zac," Carlisle said. "We'll be there later on. Is that okay?"

"Who's we?"

"Me and Steph."

"Does Stephanie know the whole thing? About the atoll, I mean?"

"Yes." Carlisle was growing more concerned.

"Okay. Just her, no one else. I'll see you at the office around two. Don't come before then. I have to get some sleep."

Carlisle said goodbye, sitting with the receiver still hanging loosely in his hand.

"What's happened?" Stephanie said.

"I don't know. He wouldn't say. He's been in the hospital. He's out now. He sounds pretty uptight, though."

He replaced the receiver carefully, seeing the sunlight in

her hair, smelling the freshness of her as she put her arms around his neck.

Letting the housecoat slip from her shoulders, Stephanie kissed him gently on the mouth. "I know it's important to see Zac," she whispered. "But we don't have to leave straight away, do we?"

He took her arms from around his neck, picked her up and carried her back to the bedroom.

Eva came hurrying from the workshop while Carlisle was still paying for the taxi.

"Oh, Mr. Carlisle and Miss Stephanie." She paused for breath. "I'm sorry. I was supposed to meet you at the airport but I didn't know what flight you were on. You should have telephoned."

"It's okay," Carlisle said. "I wasn't sure you'd be here on a Sunday."

"Even on Sundays someone has to look after that stupid man." Eva pointed upstairs. "I have to take him to the hospital last night as soon as he arrives home. He says he is fine but he can hardly walk and he looked real bad. Now he is drinking."

"How is he today?" Carlisle asked.

"I don't know, Mr. Carlisle. He is tired, I think. And angry at everyone. He's been waiting for you." Eva hesitated. "If you and Miss Stephanie are going to be here, would you mind if I went home for a while? Zac says I can take the jeep."

"You carry on." Carlisle smiled at her. "We'll look after Zac."

"Hey," Brennan called from the top of the stairs. He wore a T-shirt and a pair of filthy white shorts. In one hand he held a glass, in the other he carried a bottle of scotch. "Where the hell have you been?"

Carlisle waved a greeting. He had seen the bandage on Brennan's leg. "What's the rush?"

"I'll tell you. Come on up."

Eva touched Carlisle's arm. "You stop him drinking too much of that stuff, Mr. Carlisle."

"I'll try." He followed Stephanie up the stairs.

Brennan's office was littered with newspapers and the atmosphere was so thick with cigarette smoke it was difficult to see across the room. In its cage on top of the air-conditioning unit the mongoose was asleep. Or possibly, Carlisle thought, it had expired from lack of air.

Stephanie coughed her way into the office.

"Here." Brennan offered her a glass of scotch.

"No thanks," she said. "Zac, it's dreadful in here. Can you open a window?"

"Sure, if you don't mind getting hot." Brennan turned up the fan on the air conditioner, then jammed open the window behind his desk.

"What's wrong with your leg?" Carlisle asked.

"Bit of an accident on my holiday. Some bastard tried to kill me."

"Jesus." Carlisle stared at him. "You're not joking, are you?"

"You bet your sweet life I'm not." Brennan sat down. "You have no idea what's going on down there at Mururoa. I don't think your friend Tumahai knew either. Not when he came here."

"Does he know now?" Carlisle said.

"His daughter does. If it wasn't for her I'd still be on the goddamned atoll." Brennan paused. "In a box. The French aren't taking any chances."

"You're okay, though?" Stephanie said. "Except for your leg."

"Yeah." Brennan started rolling a cigarette. "They killed someone else instead."

Her expression changed. "Not Tumahai."

Brennan shook his head. "No, but I tell you—it's been pretty rough. I was only there four and a half days but in that time two guys were murdered."

"My God," Carlisle said. "Why?"

"Sit down and I'll give you the whole thing." After he had drained his glass of scotch, Brennan lit his cigarette. "Then you can tell me what the hell to do about it."

He started speaking more deliberately, describing Martine's first visit to his hotel before going on to outline everything he had learned during his visit to the atoll. For much of the time Carlisle remained silent, concentrating particularly on Brennan's description of the octopus at Giselle and only once asking questions to obtain more information on the clay layer.

Stephanie too was quiet, frowning while she listened to Zac explain how, on his third night, he had gone to collect the spare transducers, leaving Taufa to switch on the receiver. On hearing Brennan's account of the explosion she became visibly upset and for several seconds refused to look at him.

"You're sure it wasn't just a warning," Carlisle said. "To frighten you off."

"No chance," Brennan grunted. "You didn't see it blow. I reckon half the receiver must have been packed with high explosive. If I'd been any closer I'd be dead." He rolled himself another cigarette and lit it. "Let me finish—it gets worse." He carried on talking, this time explaining what Martine had been forced to do on the night before his escape from the atoll.

When he had finished, Carlisle's face was grim.

"Oh, Zac," Stephanie said. "It's awful. I can't believe things like that are really happening on Mururoa."

"They're happening, all right. I told you, the French aren't playing games." Brennan raised his bandaged leg. "What do you think this is?"

"Christ, what an experience," Carlisle said. "Tumahai

couldn't have known what he was doing when he came here. He was only talking about one cavern."

"Well, he knows now," Brennan said. "Or he should. Martine was going to try to see him right away." He paused. "Not that his people can do much anymore. It's too big a problem for them now."

"Tumahai won't even go to the press," Carlisle said. "What can he give them?"

"Not a thing." Brennan drew on his cigarette. "Two men are dead and poor old Tumahai's got nothing for his time or his money."

Stephanie stood up. "I don't think the money matters to him, Zac. Anyway, you've given most of it back." She placed a hand on Carlisle's shoulder. "Do you believe Zac's right about the atoll?"

Carlisle glanced up at her. "Yes, I do. I think the French are close to causing an ecological disaster—a big one—worse than anything you can imagine. If enough radioactive iodine, strontium and cesium compounds get into the marine food chain, most of the fish in that part of the Pacific are going to be contaminated with the stuff."

"And they'll be too dangerous for anyone to eat?" she said.

Carlisle nodded. "You saw those photos of newborn babies. There won't be a fishing industry—it won't exist. Think what that'll do to some of the small countries in the South Pacific. A lot of them rely on fish. Their economies will just fold up. Not to mention their main food source."

"It'll be worse than that," Brennan said. "There are Japanese fishing fleets down there. I saw Taiwanese and Korean ships, too."

"The French won't keep something like that secret," Stephanie said. "Surely they won't."

"It's worth a try," Brennan answered. "If they've found cracks and fractures right through the base of the atoll everywhere they've looked, like I think they have, they've only got two choices—keep quiet or spend billions of dollars trying to seal the caverns."

"You can't keep a mess of that size quiet for long," Carlisle said. "Three or four years ago Australia and New Zealand put a team of scientists on Mururoa. They didn't find any radioactivity in the water then, but you can bet your life they still have ships monitoring it."

"Zac," Stephanie interrupted. "It's not impossible for the French to fix the atoll, is it? If they can find enough money."

Brennan wasn't sure. "Speed's the problem," he said. "Seventy-odd test sites at around three thousand tons of concrete for each cavern on an atoll in the middle of nowhere. How the hell can they do that in a hurry by themselves?"

She sat down again. "I don't know."

"Nor do the CEP," Brennan snorted.

"So you never contacted Tumahai before you left?" Carlisle said.

"No. I told Martine we'd phone if we had any ideas. She gave me what she calls a safe number."

"We could try the newspapers here," Stephanie said. "Or go to one of the government departments in Honolulu."

"Maybe." Carlisle was thinking. "Zac, I want to hear it all over again. Draw me pictures of the worst core samples and tell me what the color of the basalt was. Then I need everything you can remember about the pipework they've built over that test site you worked on."

"Giselle," Stephanie said.

"Right." Carlisle smiled at her. "If I know how far out they're trying to seal the coral I might be able to calculate a rough leakage rate for the cavern."

"Time's getting on," Stephanie said.

"We don't have to fly back to Oahu tonight, do we?"

She shook her head. "No, not as long as you don't mind

being late for work tomorrow. It doesn't matter to me anymore. I resigned, remember?"

Brennan poured three glasses of scotch. "I am wounded, Steph has resigned, so it's all up to you, John, old buddy."

"Thanks." Carlisle took one of the glasses. "I'm supposed to be making sure you don't drink yourself insensible. Eva asked me."

"Eva hasn't got a hole in her leg." Brennan grinned and laid a fresh pad of paper on his desk. "The hospital said go home, take it easy and have a couple of drinks." He began sketching. "Okay, this is what the pipework looks like."

For the next four hours, facing each other across the desk, Brennan and Carlisle exchanged opinions on the atoll's structure, arguing over the likely extent of subterranean faulting, discussing the possibility of liquid concrete permeating through cracks in the basalt and trying to decide whether there was any other way to seal the caverns.

With the scotch gone and Stephanie on her third delivery of coffee, she finally told them to stop.

"You're doing what you always do," she said.

"What's that?" Carlisle stretched.

"You've got all tangled up in the geology instead of concentrating on the problem."

He considered the accusation. "You can't solve a geological problem unless you understand the geology," he said. "I can't, anyway." He went to switch on the light. It was dark outside and the office was beginning to cool.

"If you want more coffee I'll have to go out and buy some," Stephanie said.

"Coffee won't do it," Carlisle said. "We need an easier problem."

The mongoose had woken up. It was standing rattling the door of the cage with its paws.

"Charlie wants to stretch his legs," Carlisle said. "He's probably bored."

"Or hungry." Brennan went to look. "I haven't seen him do this before."

"Maybe Eva taught him while you were away." Stephanie stopped collecting dirty cups. "Zac, can you smell something?"

Brennan sniffed. "Diesel," he said. "Gasoline and diesel. I'd better check downstairs. I'll only be a second."

He had nearly reached the door when it burst open in his face, throwing him backward into the room.

In the doorway stood three men.

"What the hell—" Carlisle stopped suddenly. One of the men carried a revolver.

Stephanie, too, had seen the gun. The cups she'd been holding lay broken on the floor and her eyes were frightened.

As Carlisle helped Brennan to his feet, the man with the gun stepped into the office. He was tall with a thin face and dark wavy hair.

"Oh my God," Stephanie breathed. She scrambled over to Carlisle.

Without saying anything, Brennan wiped blood from the corner of his mouth.

"Mr. Brennan." The man spoke with a soft accent. "Please stand over there with your friends." He moved the barrel of his gun.

Brennan joined Stephanie and Carlisle by the air conditioner.

"My name is Lefay. The names of my colleagues are Soufrin and Lobrutto. They will remain where they are while I speak with you." Keeping his eyes on Brennan, he wedged the door open with part of a drilling head. "You will make no noise."

"Who are you?" Carlisle shouted angrily. "What the hell do you think you're doing coming in here with a gun?"

"Hold on, John." Brennan spat out more blood. "I've got a nasty idea I know who these guys are."

"Then my introduction was unnecessary," Lefay said. "And, unlike Mr. Carlisle, perhaps you, Mr. Brennan, understand the reason for my visit."

"You're DGSE," Brennan said quietly. "You're from the DGSE, aren't you?"

"Very good." Lefay's face was expressionless.

Because the Frenchman had admitted working for the DGSE so readily and because he had not hesitated to reveal his name, Brennan was already very nervous.

"Look, you can't just come in here like this." Carlisle's voice was raised. "You're out of your mind. I don't care who you are or where you're from. This is the United States, not France. You're in the wrong country. You can't use a gun here."

"Really, Mr. Carlisle." Lefay raised his eyebrows. "Your logic intrigues me."

"What do you want?" Brennan said. With the door open, the smell of gasoline was stronger.

"I am here on a simple mission to ask questions. You will please tell me what you have learned as a result of your visit to Mururoa."

"Nothing," Brennan said.

"I see. And do you also have nothing to say, Mr. Carlisle?"

Carlisle remained silent.

"Without wishing to upset Miss Tyrrel more than necessary, let me make your position clear." Lefay shifted the revolver in his hand. "I am not offering you an option."

"Is that a threat?" Carlisle asked.

"Indeed it is. You see, Mr. Carlisle, we are already aware of all your recent activities. For example, we know Tumahai visited you at the university. From phone calls we made to Miss Tyrrel at your office we learned that Tumahai subsequently met Mr. Brennan here on Maui and, of course, we know a good deal about Mr. Brennan's illegal business in Mururoa." Lefay paused. "Copies of the reports Tumahai brought to Hawaii were retrieved in small pieces from your garbage, Mr. Carlisle; we have film from the camera Mr. Brennan used on the atoll and we have a number of these."

Taking a transducer from his pocket, Lefay rolled it across the desk. "This, I believe, is one of several which were not employed during the concreting of the first cavern."

Brennan's stomach was churning. With the whole network of French intelligence on their backs, they'd never had a chance. Outclassed from the very beginning, Tumahai had dragged them into a swamp where men like Lefay were paid to bury anything that got in the way of the French testing program.

The DGSE knew everything, he thought bitterly, every damn thing that had happened from day one. Which meant Lefay knew about Martine. Or did he?

"Okay," Brennan said. "So I went to Mururoa. So what?"

Lefay's eyes narrowed. "It is not quite that straightforward, is it? In order to leave the atoll undetected you killed a man, Mr. Brennan. A man called Drollet. The knife wound in the body was discovered too late for us to apprehend you but your action indicates a determination to escape at any cost. In the opinion of my department, you would not kill unless you had secured information prejudicial to the interests of my government. I am here to discover if that is indeed the case."

They don't know about Martine, Brennan decided. Not yet they don't. "Stop being so bloody sanctimonious," he said. "Your people killed Taufa and you damn near killed me."

Lefay ignored the remark. "I require confirmation of two things," he said. "First, you will explain what you have learned of the CEP fallback position in regard to the reported typhoon sightings in the South Pacific and second, you will tell me to whom this information has been given."

"Go to hell," Brennan said. "Someone's feeding you a

lot of crap. I don't know anything about typhoons in the Pacific. Neither does John or Stephanie. Sure we were trying to help Tumahai, but your guys on the atoll screwed things up for us. We've got nothing and you know damn well we've got nothing."

Lefay beckoned to the men in the doorway. "Tie them," he said. "All of them."

"Back off," Carlisle said. "You're not tying up anyone." He moved in front of Stephanie.

The Frenchman studied him dispassionately. He threaded a small silencer onto the barrel of his gun. "Mr. Carlisle, you are not thinking clearly. I can shoot you in the kneecaps or in the stomach. It is my choice."

Carlisle gripped the back of a chair. "Leave Stephanie alone, Lefay. She's got nothing to do with this."

His eyes on Carlisle, Lefay went slowly to the air-conditioning unit, raised his gun and shot the mongoose through the head. The animal collapsed kicking in its cage, with blood dripping from its nose.

Gasping, Stephanie put her arms around Carlisle. He could feel her shaking.

Beside her, Brennan's mind was working furiously. Why were typhoon sightings so important to Lefay? How were they connected with the fallback position? Even though Martine had mentioned the word *fallback,* she neither understood what it meant nor what it was, and they had never discussed it. He tried to think.

A guess was their only chance, Brennan decided. Some kind of lucky guess. "I'll tell you," he said. "But let the girl go."

"Hold out your hands," Lefay instructed.

Slowly Brennan did as he was told, allowing the two other DGSE agents to bind his wrists with rope. Soufrin and Lobrutto were men with coarser features than Lefay's, but they wore expensive business suits like his, and both had holsters inside their jackets.

Brennan feared the worst. The situation was deteriorating by the minute and, unless he could come up with a plausible lie, he hardly dared imagine what might happen next. Carlisle was evidently still ready to fight if he had to, but Stephanie was already too terrified to speak.

"John," Brennan said. "Don't do anything stupid. It'll be okay."

While Lobrutto attended to Stephanie, Carlisle eventually permitted the man called Soufrin to lash his wrists together.

Stephanie was trembling so badly that Lobrutto swore at her.

"*Non,*" Lefray said sharply.

"Look," Brennan said. "I didn't get the idea this typhoon thing is any big deal."

"Tie the girl to that column," Lefay said. "Then bring the men here."

With sweat pouring down inside his shirt, Carlisle watched more rope being passed round Stephanie's waist and ankles.

"Good." Lefay perched himself on the edge of the desk. "Now then, Mr. Carlisle, what is the CEP's fallback strategy?"

Carlisle stared at him helplessly. "I've never heard of it."

"Mr. Brennan?"

Brennan shrugged. "I told you. Tumahai didn't say a lot."

The Frenchman nodded at his colleagues.

At once Lobrutto took hold of Stephanie's blouse and ripped it open. Underneath she wore nothing. Tears rolling down her face, she tried ineffectually to free herself.

"Well, well." Lefay drew the palm of his hand lightly across her nipples. What do you have to say now, Mr. Carlisle? Shall we add inscription on Miss Tyrrel's breasts with the end of a cigarette or do you prefer to answer my questions?"

By now Brennan had reached an inescapable conclusion. Even if they could satisfy Lefay, the events of tonight were already too serious for the DGSE to walk away from.

Whether Lefay obtained answers or not was unimportant. The DGSE had only come to Hawaii for one reason. They were here to clean up.

Carlisle was swearing, struggling to untie his wrists.

"John," Brennan said. "I figure this is a one-way road." It was too late to worry about Lefay swallowing a lie.

Gritting his teeth, Carlisle nodded.

"So there's only one way to go down, right?"

Again Carlisle nodded. His eyes were on Stephanie.

"Take the men out," Lefay commanded. "Now, out onto the stairs—quickly."

"John, no," Stephanie pleaded. "For God's sake tell them. Make Zac tell them. Don't leave me—please."

"Here." Lefay gave Lobrutto a handkerchief. "Put that in her mouth. It will burn with the rope."

"Go," Carlisle yelled. He hurled himself at Soufrin.

Simultaneously Brennan kicked out at Lefay's gun.

Both maneuvers were unsuccessful. On his knees at the top of the stairway, Soufrin parried another attack from Carlisle while he scrambled to his feet. Then he slammed his gun hard against Carlisle's face.

Lefay was more restrained. The kick had failed to dislodge the gun from his hand—a gun now leveled at the center of Brennan's forehead.

Lobrutto had finished gagging Stephanie. On Lefay's instructions he helped push Brennan and Carlisle downstairs and escort them into the ground-floor workshop.

Even in the dark Brennan could see upturned cans of fuel.

"Although I am inclined to believe you may indeed know nothing, I shall ask you once more," Lefay said. "What has Daniel Tumahai learned of the typhoon from his people on the atoll or from traitors inside France?"

Dizzy from the blow to his head, Carlisle forced his mind to work. The smell of gasoline was overpowering and he, too, had seen the cans.

"Well?" Lefay prompted.

"Listen, Lefay," Brennan said. "From where I'm standing I don't think you're about to do a deal. What happens if we tell you what you want to know?"

"Then we shall immediately release Miss Tyrrel and you and Mr. Carlisle may go free. Surely that is obvious to you?"

"Bullshit," Brennan said.

"Hang on, Zac." Carlisle knew he had to improvise. "Tumahai told me about the typhoon when he came to Honolulu. I tape-recorded the whole conversation but I don't remember exactly what he said. The tape's in my office at the university."

"What parts do you remember?"

"Only the word—something about a storm on the atoll."

"Ah, I see." Lefay smiled coldly. He motioned for Soufrin and Lobrutto to leave. "Mr. Carlisle, after recent events in Eastern Europe you may consider it unnecessary for my country to maintain an independent nuclear deterrent. But you are wrong. The reunification of Germany is a dangerous possibility and the Soviet Union could easily revert to its old ways if the Russian economy continues to deteriorate. For these reasons, France will not stop nuclear testing in the Pacific and I can assure you my government will not permit people like you to interfere with its policy. You have meddled in something you neither appreciate nor understand."

"Never mind the political crap," Brennan said. "What about the tape?"

"Goodbye, gentlemen." Lefay backed away. Before either Brennan or Carlisle could do anything to stop him he had tossed a lighted match into a pool of gasoline. For an instant the flames stayed low to the ground, flickering in the darkness.

"Get out," Brennan yelled. "Rush the bastard."

But they moved too late. In front of them with a huge roar, the wall became a solid sheet of flame. Through it there was a glimpse of Lefay disappearing out the door.

More flames spread across the workshop floor, setting fire to wooden benches and igniting puddles of spilled diesel oil. In a few seconds all the walls were burning.

"Drilling rig," Brennan yelled. "We'll drive out. Get down—crawl."

Surrounded by fire, shouting Stephanie's name above the noise, Carlisle refused to move. Flames started licking at the ceiling.

"Crawl, you bastard." Brennan hit him in the face.

This time Carlisle responded. On their bellies, hands still tied, they began worming their way over to the truck. Ten feet from it, a blazing portion of the roof collapsed in front of them. At the same time the side wall of the workshop exploded inward. Wreathed in smoke, briefly, the nose of the jeep appeared.

Gasping for air, the back of his T-shirt smoldering, Brennan grabbed Carlisle and pointed. They ran headlong for the gap.

Outside, the jeep was accelerating as Eva prepared to ram the wall again. She saw them, braking heavily before jumping down to help.

"Hold on to John," Brennan coughed. "For Christ's sake don't let him go." He ripped off his T-shirt.

Still yelling for Stephanie, Carlisle was fighting to escape. Over the workshop, most of the office was already gone and the one remaining wall was engulfed in flame.

"I can't stop him," Eva shouted. "Quick."

Seizing a wrench from the jeep in both hands, Brennan brought it down on Carlisle's head.

SIX

BRENNAN opened two cans of beer and took them with him out onto the verandah. As usual at this time of day, a breeze was coming up the valley from the sea, rustling the leaves on the ironwood tree and tinkling the wind chimes that hung in the doorway to the living room.

Lying motionless in the hammock, Carlisle was staring into space.

"Here." Brennan offered him a can.

Carlisle shook his head.

"Have one. It's pretty hot out here. You'll dehydrate."

"I don't want a beer." Climbing out of the hammock, Carlisle went to sit on the verandah rail.

"Do you want to talk?" Brennan said.

"What about?"

Brennan controlled his frustration. "Look," he said. "Whether you like it or not we have to make some decisions. We can't go on staying here for a start."

"Eva says she doesn't mind."

"This isn't Eva's place, it's her brother's. That's not the point anyway, is it?"

Ignoring him, Carlisle continued staring down the valley.

"John, listen to me. I know how you feel but you have to let go of it. You and Steph were only going together for what—a week—a few days. You can't let one week screw up your whole life." Brennan spoke quietly.

"It was ten months," Carlisle said. "I knew her for ten months."

"She's dead, John."

Carlisle swung round. "She was killed. There's a difference."

Brennan had seen this expression on his face before. In the four days they'd been here in the Kipahulu valley, Carlisle had changed. Not just because of what had happened to Stephanie, Brennan thought. It was everything. The realization that men like Lefay existed, a sudden awareness of a darker, more sinister world where the lives of ordinary people were expendable at the whim of governments. And it was the atoll—a place Carlisle had barely thought about two weeks ago but now a place he would never be able to get out of his mind.

"We've got to talk," Brennan said.

"Because the DGSE could be looking for us or because you want to get on with your life?"

Brennan was careful not to rise to the remark. "We don't know if the DGSE are looking for us or not," he said. "My guess is Lefay believes we're dead. But that's not what we need to talk about. We have to decide what we're going to do about all of this—the whole thing."

"I've already told you." Carlisle reached for one of the cans of beer. "Don't you believe me?"

"Sure. I believe that's how you feel right now."

"But you think I'll get over it? Settle down or something?"

"I don't know." Brennan didn't want a repeat of the argument they'd had yesterday.

"You're wrong. I don't care if it takes me the rest of my life, I'm going to find Lefay."

Although, in the aftermath of the fire, Carlisle's reaction was understandable, Brennan knew it was essential to redirect the conversation. Indulging in ideas of vengeance was one thing, deciding practically what to do next was far less easy.

Carlisle drank the beer without stopping. He crushed the can and threw it away. "I'm not going to leave this alone, Zac."

"You don't have to. But you can let Tumahai handle the heavy stuff." Brennan prevented Carlisle from interrupting. "I don't mean by himself. Tumahai's people understand the rules—believe me, they do. All we have to do is help them. If we can supply the right ammunition they'll sink the DGSE and Lefay'll go down at the same time."

Carlisle shook his head. "When the DGSE blew up that Greenpeace ship in New Zealand to stop it going to Mururoa, they killed a guy. And what happened? Nothing. The DGSE had their wrists slapped and a couple of their agents were given a holiday on Howe Island. It didn't even slow the French down. What the hell can Tumahai do now that he couldn't do then?"

"The French weren't in trouble with the atoll back then," Brennan answered. "Things have changed. Right now they're scared. They wouldn't have sent Lefay here unless they're desperate to keep the problem secret. They're frightened we'll make big waves."

"You can't make big waves without a big paddle. We can't help Tumahai because we've got nothing he can use."

Brennan was encouraged. For the first time Carlisle was at least attempting to discuss matters unemotionally. "Yes we do," he said. "I think we've tripped over something pretty important."

"These bloody typhoon sightings?"

"Yeah. Not even the French are stupid enough to do what they've done unless this fallback position Lefay kept talking about is real critical to them."

"You're guessing," Carlisle grunted. "We don't know what it is and you said Tumahai and his daughter don't know either."

"Martine never mentioned typhoon sightings. She just asked me to see if I could figure out what a fallback position could be. She thought the CEP had dreamed up another way of sealing the caverns—some kind of last resort if the concreting doesn't work."

"Okay. So we tell Tumahai that typhoon sightings are important," Carlisle said. "Big deal. What the hell can he do?"

"Let's find out." Brennan spoke carefully again. "Neither of us are going to get very far by ourselves, are we? And I'm not about to let you go off half cocked by yourself." He began rolling a cigarette.

"What are you going to do? Smack me over the head again?"

"It worked last time. How's the head this morning?"

"Lousy." Carlisle touched the bump. "It hurts more than my face where that bastard Soufrin hit me."

"Walking wounded," Brennan said. "Me with one leg and you with dents in your head."

"At least my arms are better." Carlisle examined the scabs covering the rope grooves around his wrists. "You know, I can't understand the way you're handling this. I keep waiting for you to get angry—start yelling or something."

"I had a tough week on Mururoa first," Brennan said. "I saw Taufa die and I saw Martine go out with a knife to kill a guy. My yelling's all done. I'm more numb than anything."

"How numb?"

Brennan stared at him. "Look, John," he said. "I'm not going to forget Steph either. Don't get the idea I can handle this any better than you can. I just figure that whatever we do we need to do it right. We're only alive by accident. If Eva had decided to go back to the office two minutes later than she did, we wouldn't even be here. We've made a big enough mess of things so far, don't you think?"

"And phoning Tumahai is a smart first step?"

"Maybe. What have we got to lose?"

In the distance a dust cloud was traveling up the valley. Brennan went into the house, returning with a pair of binoculars. Steadying them against the corner pillar of the verandah he endeavored to track the approaching vehicle.

"Is it Eva?" Carlisle asked.

"Don't know. It's a bit early for her. I can't see anything except dust." Brennan continued watching. Of the four other properties serviced by the dirt road that led from the coast, only one was occupied at present and he had seen the four-wheel-drive Nissan belonging to the owners go out less than half an hour ago.

Carlisle stood up. "If it's Eva's brother he'll be surprised to find us here."

Brennan grunted. "So long as it's not someone else." Through the trees there was a flash of red and he saw the distinctive shape of a roll bar. "It's okay," he said. "It's Eva."

A few seconds later the jeep came bouncing down the driveway. What remained of the front bumper was dragging on one of the front tires and, where the paintwork had been scorched by the fire, spots of rust were already beginning to appear.

"Hi." Eva waved to them.

Switching off the engine, she got out and gingerly removed her hat and a transparent plastic raincoat. Both the hat and the coat were smothered in fine road dust. After stamping more dust from her shoes she climbed the steps onto the verandah.

"Rotten drive," Brennan said.

Eva grinned. "No good for my best dress and no good for me."

Carlisle went to fetch her a Coke. When he returned she was sprawling in a chair with her shoes off.

"Oh thank you, Mr. Carlisle." She took the can. "It was better you stayed here."

"Why?" Carlisle had made the decision not to attend the funeral several days ago.

"The police were looking for you. And for Zac. They ask me questions."

Brennan was not altogether surprised. Despite the fierceness of the fire it would have been easy enough for the police to determine how many people had died in the building. "What kind of questions?" he asked.

"They see the way the diesel and gas cans are lying on the ground so they think the fire is on purpose."

"And they believe we did it?" Carlisle asked.

"Maybe." Eva drank some Coke. "There is one man who spoke to me—a detective from Honolulu. Because Miss Stephanie worked for you, Mr. Carlisle, he said it is strange you are not at the funeral."

"What did you say?" Brennan was worried. This was the very thing they'd talked about last night. Except that last night they hadn't imagined the police would move so quickly.

"I lie. I say you are both on business on the mainland. In Los Angeles." She paused. "I think they start looking harder for you pretty soon."

"Damn," Carlisle said. Like Brennan he hadn't foreseen events overtaking them at this speed.

"You go to the police here on Maui and tell them what happened," Eva said. "It is safer, I think."

"And spend six months trying to explain something no one's going to believe." Brennan was equally concerned about the DGSE. By now Lefay, too, could have learned that Stephanie was the only victim of the fire.

"My brother has other houses," Eva said. "On the Big Island. You go there. I take you. There is one house with no road to it."

"Your brother sounds like an interesting guy," Carlisle said. "What does he do?"

"Don't ask." Brennan already knew.

She smiled. "He grows a little pakalolo. But you don't tell anyone, Mr. Carlisle."

Carlisle was silent.

"Well, he won't be too pleased if the police start trampling all over his plantations looking for us, will he?" Brennan paused. "I hope like hell no one thought of tailing you, Eva."

"I check for cars on my drive back here. There is nothing behind me from Kahului. I am very careful to look."

"What's the time now?" Brennan said. "I still haven't got a damn watch."

Carlisle checked. "Four o'clock. Why?"

"I'm going to make that call—to the number Martine gave me. Tahiti's on the same time as us, so Tumahai could be there."

"If he is, ask him to call off Eva's detective," Carlisle said sarcastically. "That shouldn't be too hard."

"You might be surprised. Tumahai's a smart old guy and he has friends in Hawaii. Have you got a better idea?"

"No." Carlisle shook his head.

"Right then." Brennan turned to Eva. "Is it okay if I use the phone?"

"Sure it is. Call who you want." Eva pushed herself out of her chair. "I go for a long shower while you and Mr. Carlisle do some thinking, eh?" She picked up her shoes and shuffled off barefoot.

"I'll get the number," Brennan said. He followed Eva into the house.

Even though Carlisle doubted the wisdom of phoning Daniel Tumahai, on balance, he thought, Zac was probably right. In the absence of any other ideas, what harm could it do? And maybe Zac had been right about something else too—about the need to discuss the future. In the last half hour Carlisle realized he had been functioning almost normally. It was a sign perhaps—a sign that it was possible after all to dispel the bitterness he had begun to believe might never go away.

"Hey." Brennan was calling to him from the window. "Do you want to listen?"

Carlisle went into the living room and watched Brennan push the buttons on the phone.

"I bet you twenty bucks we're out of luck," Brennan said. "I don't have a good feeling about this."

There was a series of clicks on the line followed by the sound of the receiver being lifted.

"Hello," Brennan said cautiously.

"Oui?" A girl's voice answered.

"This is Zac Brennan. Martine, is that you?" He was certain it was.

"Oh, hello. Yes, it's me." Her voice was brittle. "Where are you calling from, Brennan?"

"Hawaii."

"You got home all right, then."

"Yeah, I'm fine." A minor exaggeration, Brennan thought. "We've had trouble, though. The DGSE were here. They killed someone."

The line was silent.

"Martine?" Brennan queried.

"I'm here. Are you calling from somewhere safe?"

"Yes. I want to speak to your father. Is he there?"

There was a long pause. "My father died yesterday morning in a car accident." She spoke very quietly.

"Oh, Jesus." Brennan could not disguise his shock. "Hell, I'm sorry."

"What's wrong?" Carlisle whispered.

Brennan covered the mouthpiece. "Hang on. I'll tell you in a minute." He tried to think what to say.

"Have you seen anyone from the DGSE?" She asked the question so quietly he could barely hear her.

"Yes. A real bastard called Lefay. He thinks we know something we shouldn't."

"Oh." She paused again. "I don't believe my father's death was an accident."

This time he was more cautious with his reply. "Martine," he said. "John Carlisle and I are in trouble here. So are you by the sound of it. What about trying to figure out something between us? Can you talk now?"

"I'm staying on Rangiroa. That's where this phone is. I can't go back to the atoll in case they're looking for me too. I don't think I can do anything, but I can talk for as long as you like."

"Okay. I'll tell you what's happened here first." He put his hand over the receiver again and spoke to Carlisle. "Look, this'll take a while. Why don't you go and have another beer?"

Knowing Zac would be uncomfortable talking about the fire while he remained in the room, Carlisle wandered back onto the verandah. Eva was there, sitting on the rail, drying her hair.

"Have you finished?" she asked.

"No, Zac's still talking to the girl."

"Mr. Carlisle?"

"Yes." He glanced at her.

"You talk to me. You tell me everything how you feel. This is a good time for you to talk, I think."

Unwillingly at first, but finding that the words came more easily once he had overcome his initial reservations, Carlisle told her. He was still speaking twenty minutes later when Brennan rejoined them.

"Am I interrupting?" Zac was evidently pleased about something.

Carlisle shook his head. "We've finished. We were just talking about Steph."

Brennan's expression changed.

"It's okay," Carlisle said quickly.

"I make a salad," Eva said. "You call me when you want to eat." She wrapped the towel around her head. "Mr. Carlisle," she said. "You remember what I say—you don't ever stop trying to remember."

Carlisle smiled his thanks as she turned to leave. Until this afternoon he hadn't understood Zac's affection for Eva. Now he did.

"Smart lady," Brennan grunted. "Don't you think?"

Carlisle looked at him. "Very smart," he said.

"Well, we're in business." Brennan sat down and took out his tobacco. "I've got what I reckon is a pretty good idea." He paused. "All you have to do is solve a puzzle."

"What kind of puzzle?"

"Listen to this." Telling him first about Daniel Tumahai, Brennan moved on rapidly. "I know what typhoon sightings are."

Carlisle raised his eyebrows slightly. He said nothing.

"French Polynesia doesn't have typhoons." Brennan was still speaking quickly. "Down there they call them cyclones."

"Hang on." Carlisle was thinking about Tumahai. "Slow down, will you? What do you mean his daughter doesn't believe Tumahai was killed in a car accident?"

"She doesn't know for sure. Sometime yesterday afternoon she arrived home and heard that his car had gone over a cliff about twenty-five kilometers outside Papeete. A couple of tourists found him."

"What makes her think it wasn't an accident?"

Brennan shrugged. "Hunch—intuition. I don't know. I guess after what happened on the atoll she's fairly suspicious, but she said her father had no reason to go out anywhere and he left his hat behind in the house. Do you remember that damn hat of his?"

"Not much in the way of evidence, is it?"

"How much do you want? You've seen the DGSE in action. So have I, so has Martine. At the same time as the French were making sure there weren't any loose ends here they were tidying up in Tahiti. Tumahai was more of a threat to them than any of us—or at least the DGSE thought he was."

"Oh, Christ," Carlisle said suddenly. "We could've warned him. We could have phoned two days ago."

"If we'd thought of it." Brennan finished rolling his cigarette. He let it hang unlit between his lips. "We were kind of busy with our own problems."

"What's his daughter going to do?"

"Keep her head down. She's gone to this other island—Rangiroa. Apparently she's heard of Lefay. He's a DGSE field agent from the base in Papeete."

Carlisle felt the muscles in his throat tighten. Even the mention of Lefay brought it all back. He remembered the Frenchman's eyes.

"Does Martine think Lefay's after her, too?" he said.

"She doesn't know. She's pretty scared, though. More scared now—after what I told her. Do you want to hear about this typhoon thing, or not?"

"Yes. Go on." Carlisle wondered if Lefay was already back in Tahiti.

"Typhoons aren't typhoons," Brennan said. "And they're not cyclones, either. They're goddamn submarines. Soviet submarines. How does that grab you?"

So far, the information did not grab Carlisle at all.

"Typhoon-class Russian subs," Brennan continued. "The bastards have been hanging around the atoll monitoring the tests—or one of them has. The French have seen it, so have other people. Martine said there was a sighting by a U.S. frigate, and the Australian navy reported seeing the same one about a month ago."

"That's crazy," Carlisle said. "Lefay was talking about Typhoon sightings as part of the French fallback position to fix up the atoll. What's he going to do—ask the Russians to take bits of their submarines and stuff them into the caverns to stop the leaks?"

"That's the puzzle. What you have to figure out. I know it doesn't make any sense. Martine thinks it's crazy, too."

"Why the hell should I be able to figure it out?" Carlisle said.

"Because you're smarter than I am, and because, in case you've forgotten, we're stuck here on an island."

"What's that got to do with it?" Carlisle's mood was worsening again.

Standing up, Brennan balanced himself on his good leg and kicked a beer can off the verandah. "I'll tell you. You can spend as long as you like hanging around here or hiding out in some other house that belongs to Eva's brother on the Big Island. But in the end the police are going to run you down. And once that happens, you're finished. Stephanie's dead. It's done and there's nothing you can do to bring her back. If you want to loll around feeling sorry for yourself that's fine, but don't expect any sympathy from me. I thought you wanted to find Lefay."

"I do."

He didn't carry on as though Carlisle hadn't said anything—he answered him. "No, you don't. It's real easy to talk about it, though, isn't it? Pretend you'll find a way when you're ready. Well, you listen to me. There's a girl down there in Tahiti who's seen three quarters of her family wiped out and, right now, that bastard Lefay's probably trying to find her. And if he does find her it's going to be your fault because you don't give a shit about anything except yourself. You don't care about her any more than you care about those people in Tahiti."

For the first time in four days Carlisle was almost smiling. Even if the outburst had been contrived, Zac's attempt to provoke him had succeeded. Whether he wanted to or not Carlisle knew he had to reply.

"How long have you been planning that?" he said.

"Since I came off the phone." Brennan grinned. "There's more if you want to hear it."

"The buildup to the great Brennan idea?"

"Yeah."

"Spare me—just the idea will do."

"I figure I ought to go back to Tahiti and I think you should go with me." Brennan met his eyes. "And don't start giving me a hard time."

The possibility of visiting the atoll had occurred to Carlisle two days ago but then the idea had seemed futile and too dangerous. Tumahai had not only failed to appreciate the true extent of the damage to the atoll but grossly underestimated the French response to any interference in their affairs. As a result Tumahai and Taufa were dead. And because Zac had gone stumbling into something he had not properly understood, Stephanie too had died. To repeat the mistakes would be all too easy, Carlisle had thought. Now, with much better information—even though some of it was incomprehensible—he was less inclined to reject the idea out of hand.

"We have to get out of Honolulu first," he said. "And there'll be a problem at the other end for you. The DGSE will have your name listed on the airport computers in Tahiti. Their immigration people will jump you the minute they see your passport."

"Sure," Brennan agreed. "So we have to move fast at this end and get Martine to pull some strings for us in Papeete." He was watching Carlisle's face. "From what Eva's said I reckon it'll be another twenty-four hours before the police clamp down on the Honolulu airport."

"Have you already talked about this to Martine?"

"Yes. More or less."

"Which?" Carlisle said.

"More. She can fix things in Papeete—so she says." Brennan sensed victory. "I figured you'd hemorrhage as soon as I mentioned going to Tahiti."

"I haven't said it's a great idea." Carlisle paused. "It's a lousy idea."

"But the only one we've got—right?"

"Maybe."

"Lefay's there," Brennan said quietly. "And there's a chance we can crack this Typhoon thing. Then we'll have something to give the newspapers. You don't want to walk away from this problem with the atoll any more than I do. I know you don't."

"Do you trust this girl Martine?"

Brennan nodded.

"It's still a lousy idea," Carlisle said. "It's full of holes. What are we going to do when we get there?"

"Sort ourselves out. Move nice and easy. I said I'd call Martine back in half an hour. She's waiting to hear."

This time Carlisle's smile was genuine. "One condition," he said. "No cowboy stuff and I make the decisions."

"Sure. I can always thump you with the wrench again." Brennan was grinning. "I'll take it with me." He hurried off to make the call.

Alone on the verandah, remembering Eva's advice, Carlisle climbed back into the hammock, closed his eyes and let his mind idle. Less than a year had passed since he had wondered if his appointment to the university would turn out to be another job that led nowhere or if a fresh environment would enliven a career that had become increasingly boring to him.

A succession of impermanent relationships with more women than he cared to recall had allowed him to leave Europe with no regrets, no ties and without any preconceived notions of what he wanted to do. And, until this had happened, the move had been good for him, he thought. Ten months of sunshine and the pleasure of exploring a place where, from the moment he'd arrived, he had experienced the feeling of being somewhere he wanted to be.

Then, either by accident or because Stephanie herself had forced the issue, she had entered his life—an intrusion which, at first, he had almost resented. Now she was gone—just as he had realized he was in love with her—snatched from him by men who had displayed no more compunction in killing her than they had in killing the mongoose.

The anger came surging up inside him again. Embarking on some ill-defined crusade to stop radioactive water leaking into the Pacific had to be madness, Carlisle thought. Or was that the response from someone who had once been a geologist? A reaction to circumstances so far removed from any he could have imagined a few days ago that there was no sensible response.

"Mr. Carlisle." Eva's head appeared at the window. "Are you awake?"

"Yes." He opened his eyes.

"Zac's finished on the phone. Do you want to eat? It's ready."

"Okay, I'm coming." He slid out of the hammock, anxious to hear what Martine had said.

Inside, Brennan was already seated at the table. "All set," he said. "It's tricky but it sounds all right."

"What does?" Carlisle sat down.

"Our trip. You're going to need your passport. Where is it?"

"At home."

Brennan was thoughtful. "We'll have to pick it up on the way," he said. "Unless the police have someone watching your place."

"What about the other end?"

"I told you. It's all set. We book a flight from here to Sydney, Australia. Martine says Qantas is the best bet because a lot of their flights have stopovers in Tahiti. We get off the plane at Papeete and go to the transit lounge with everyone else. All we're given is a transit card."

"How do we get out of the lounge?"

"Two of Martine's friends will meet us in the men's room. They work at the airport. They'll have overalls for us and a couple of airport staff badges. We just walk out of the place. Security's not that tight there—I've seen what it's like."

Carlisle had spent enough time in transit lounges to know the plan was flawed. "Forget it," he said. "The plane won't be allowed to take off if they're two passengers short. There's always a head count to make sure no one's left behind."

"Ah." Brennan grinned. "That's the clever bit. These other guys board the plane with our transit cards instead of us. They'll fly on to Australia using their own passports. The head count will be the same and the other people on the plane will think we got off in Papeete. They'll just assume a couple of new passengers joined the plane for the flight from Tahiti to Sydney. It'll work like a charm."

Carlisle was beginning to believe it might.

"Well?" Brennan urged.

"How will Martine know what flight we're on?"

"We phone her before we leave. Soon as she hears, she'll make all the arrangements and book us on a plane from Papeete to Rangiroa. That's an internal route so we won't have to show passports."

"We're going to Rangiroa?" Carlisle said.

"Martine reckons that's the safest place for us to catch our breath while we try to sort out this weird thing about the Soviet submarine. I told her you're good at puzzles."

"So now you run away to another part of the world," Eva said. "This girl in Tahiti is more stupid than both of you, I think. When are you to go?"

"Ask John," Brennan said. "He's supposed to be making the decisions."

Carlisle had not forgotten the Hawaiian police or the need to collect his passport. Neither had he forgotten how rapidly their situation was changing.

"Mr. Carlisle?" Eva was waiting for his reply.

He helped himself to some of her salad, then smiled at her. "What time's the last plane out of Maui to Oahu?" he said.

Sitting with his leg wedged uncomfortably under the seat in front of him, Brennan watched the lights of Waikiki slip away beneath the wing of the big jet. It was little more than two weeks since Daniel Tumahai had accompanied him on his first visit to Tahiti—a journey that had cost Taufa, Stephanie and Tumahai their lives.

Had he known then what the cost would be, there would have been no visit, no subsequent escape from the atoll and he would not now be heading out over the Pacific bound for the islands of French Polynesia for a second time.

But the journeys were dissimilar, he decided. Tonight was a fresh start, a different journey altogether. In the seat beside him, instead of Tumahai, John Carlisle sat staring out the window and, this time, instead of the French expecting them, they would arrive unannounced, better informed and armed with a determination that came from all that had gone before.

In the hours leading up to their departure from Maui, Brennan had detected signs of improvement in his friend. At first these had been little more than brief flashes of the old Carlisle, but once they reached Oahu and had collected his passport without incident, he had become more positive and had seemed almost eager to be on his way.

Looking at him now, Brennan saw a stranger in the making—a young man still working through his bitterness but a man who was already harder and already dangerously unforgiving.

The DGSE had miscalculated, Brennan thought. And, without realizing it, in failing to complete his job, Lefay could have made a big mistake. One hell of a big mistake.

SEVEN

UNLIKE Mururoa, from the ground Rangiroa looked as sleepy as it had done from the air during the plane's approach to the island. The tiny palm-fringed terminal appeared to be deserted, showing no signs of life even after the plane had taxied off the runway to park in front of the building.

Disembarking with the handful of other passengers who had been with them on the flight from Papeete, Brennan and Carlisle walked cautiously toward an exit gate in the perimeter fence.

A solitary baggage tractor snaked across the tarmac, the driver sitting sidesaddle, engrossed in a newspaper on his lap.

Brennan's tension began to ease. Because things had gone so smoothly since their departure from Hawaii, in the latter stage of their final one-hour flight to Rangiroa he had become concerned that their luck might not hold. Now, only feet from the gate, it was nearly too late for anything to go wrong.

"What do you think?" Carlisle was still uneasy.

"Looks pretty quiet." Brennan had one eye on a uniformed gendarme standing inside the entrance to the baggage claim area. "If there was going to be trouble, we'd have run into it before now."

Outside the gate the other passengers were boarding a brightly painted open-air courtesy bus bearing the name KIA ORA HOTEL on its side.

Immediately behind the bus stood a dilapidated flatbed truck. Rust had eaten away most of the body, there was no evidence of any windshield and a few rotten wooden planks were all that remained of what had once been the deck.

The girl at the wheel suddenly waved to them. She jumped down from the cab and came to say hello.

Martine was wearing a coloured *pareu,* pulled in at her waist to form a short skirt. "Hi." She nodded at Brennan before turning to Carlisle. "I'm Martine Tumahai," she said. "*Maeva* to French Polynesia, Mr. Carlisle."

He shook hands, seeing someone who had nothing in common with the girl Zac had described to him. "My name's John," he said.

"I know. My father told me a lot about you."

"I'm sorry about your father." Carlisle searched for the correct thing to say. "He was a fine man."

"Thank you." She looked away. "He was but he didn't understand what's happening. He should never have gone to see you in Hawaii. It's his fault you're mixed up in this."

"He was only doing what he believed was right," Carlisle said.

"Yes." She glanced at him. "I wasn't sure what to expect. I thought you might be, you know—hostile." She flushed. "I'm sorry. This isn't a very good place to talk. We have to go to the village. It isn't far."

"Just as well if we're going in that." Brennan pointed at the truck.

"It's the only transport we have. You can always walk, Brennan."

"I'll take the ride." He grinned, pleased that she seemed

to have overcome her awkwardness. "I've got a hole in my leg, remember?"

"Is it better?"

"Bit stiff from being on the plane, that's all." Brennan accompanied her to the truck.

Carlisle followed behind, wondering if for some reason Zac had been less than truthful in imparting his impressions of Martine. By any standard she was stunningly attractive, Carlisle thought. And Zac had made no attempt to conceal how pleased he was to see her again.

With some difficulty, Martine wrenched open the passenger door of the truck. Hiking up her skirt she climbed into the cab. "We'll all have to squeeze in here together," she said. "I have to get in this side because the other door's welded up."

Carlisle waited for Brennan to slide across the seat before pulling himself inside and slamming the door.

"I wasn't sure if you'd come straight off the plane." She engaged the starter. "I thought you might have baggage to collect."

"Wasn't time for baggage. We left in a bit of a hurry." Brennan's voice was drowned in the roar from an unmuffled exhaust.

Narrowly missing the still driverless hotel bus, the truck lurched forward, gathering speed as Martine gunned the engine. She drove fast in the center of the road, occasionally swerving to miss potholes, clearly unconcerned at the prospect of meeting vehicles coming the other way.

Beside her, arms braced against the dashboard, Brennan was shouting something in her ear.

Pretending she couldn't hear, she ignored him, driving with one hand on the wheel while she used the other to keep her hair out of her eyes.

Carlisle was amused, recalling how Zac had used the word wildcat to describe Martine and how he'd been at pains to explain she was not at all like her father. But Zac hadn't known Tumahai as a young man, Carlisle thought. And Tumahai's daughter had grown up in a very different society—a society still fighting against the exploitation of Tahiti by the French.

The truck slowed and began traveling at a more reasonable speed.

Martine leaned across to speak to Carlisle. "It's not too bumpy for you, is it?"

He smiled. "No. Where's this village we're going to?"

"Near the Tiputa Pass. Just this side of a gap in the reef where the lagoon connects with the sea. It's a fishing village. My mother was born there."

"Was she Tahitian?" Carlisle asked.

She nodded. "A special Tahitian. The people who live on Rangiroa are all special—they're called Paumoto. My mother's family all come from here."

She returned to her driving, not speaking again until she swung the truck off onto a track leading inland toward the lagoon. The track was heavily overgrown and populated by dozens of chickens, which scattered at the truck's approach.

"Hold on," she said, "and watch out for branches coming through the windows."

After curving around a giant outcrop of rock, the track opened up onto a plateau that led down to a beach of sparkling white sand.

Clustered together near the water's edge were a number of circular, thatched-roofed huts. Farther out in the lagoon, surrounded by fishing boats, another group of similar huts were perched on stilts, their floors only one or two feet above the water.

Martine parked outside what Carlisle imagined was the village store—a ramshackle building made of rusty corrugated iron. Children came running from all directions to meet the truck.

"I know this place doesn't look much." She switched off

the engine. "But the people are lovely and hardly anyone visits here."

"It's great." Carlisle opened the door to find a sea of inquisitive young faces peering at him.

"Hi there." He got out.

There was no response from the audience.

Not until Brennan and Martine had joined him was there any change in the children's expressions.

"Say hello." Martine spoke to them.

There was a chorus of shy *Maevas* before they broke ranks and ran away giggling.

"They're not used to strangers," Martine explained. "You're a novelty."

Carlisle was staring out over the huge lagoon.

"What are you looking at?" she asked.

"Nothing. I was just thinking that this village was probably the same a hundred years ago as it is now. There's nowhere like it left in Hawaii. There hasn't been for years and years. I suppose that's why people like Robert Louis Stevenson and Gauguin used to come to Tahiti—because it doesn't change, I mean."

"Oh. I'll show you where you'll be staying." She headed off toward one of the huts on the beach.

"Some atoll," Brennan grunted. "This makes Mururoa look like L.A. What the hell are we going to be able to do if we're living in a grass hut?"

"See what Martine has to say."

Brennan grinned. "I'll tell her we need a telephone and a fax machine."

"Come on." Carlisle began walking down the beach.

She was waiting for them. "In Tahitian these cottages are called *fares,*" she said. "They're cool but that's about all. I'm sorry there isn't even any fresh water. A tanker comes every week but it only brings enough for drinking and cooking."

Carlisle ducked through the entrance. Inside it was quite

dark and smelt of wood smoke mixed with what he thought was vanilla. On a floor of freshly picked leaves were a plastic bucket and two foam mattresses.

"Will this be all right?" Martine sounded awkward.

"Look, you've got the wrong idea about me," Carlisle said. "This is fine. Why wouldn't it be?"

"Europeans don't usually come to places like this and you work at the university in Hawaii. This isn't . . ." Her voice trailed off.

He smiled at her. "Is it okay to swim in the lagoon?"

She nodded. "Here it is. But don't go out too far and keep away from the mouth of the pass. It's only a little way up the reef."

"Right." Carlisle threw his overnight bag onto one of the beds. "We'll take a quick swim to freshen up, then we'll all have a talk. Stop worrying. Zac's fine, so am I."

She turned to leave. "I just wanted you to be comfortable while you're here. I wasn't worried about Brennan."

"Well, thanks." Brennan winked at Carlisle. "Maybe you want to take this other mattress away and let me sleep on the floor?" He lay down on it, putting his hands behind his head.

"I'll see if there's some food." She drew a curtain of woven palm fronds across the entrance and disappeared.

"Well." Brennan closed his eyes. "Here we are. What do you think of Miss Tumahai?"

"I'm not sure yet. I can believe she killed that guy you told me about on Mururoa but she's not as hard-bitten as you think she is. She's even scared she's done the wrong thing bringing us here because she knows the village could get into trouble if anyone finds out we're here." Carlisle paused. "I don't think you've picked her right. Tumahai would've told me if his daughter was some kind of Tahitian terrorist."

"You didn't see her that night on the atoll. Taufa knew

her and he thought she was pretty tough." Brennan sat up. "My friend Martine is on her best behavior."

"Why?"

"God knows." Brennan grinned. "But have you ever seen anyone with eyes like those? Or with a body like that?"

Carlisle's suspicion grew. An image of Stephanie hovered at the edge of his mind. He let it stay there, making no effort either to remember or to forget. "You go easy," he said. "We've got things to do."

"Yeah." Brennan jumped off the bed and started to undress. "Come on, let's get in that water."

They returned from their swim to find Martine standing outside the fare. "I've told everyone in the village we'll eat with them this evening," she said. "So we'll just have a snack now if that's okay."

Carlisle shook the water from his hair, then sat down on a grass mat. "You don't have to go to any trouble for us, you know," he said. "If we have to stay here for a while we'll pay for our keep."

"I figured we could buy something for the village," Brennan said. "Something they need."

Her eyes flashed briefly. "With my father's money, you mean."

"Oh Jesus," Brennan muttered. "Not again." He went into the fare, reappearing with his body belt in his hand. He threw it at her feet. "Forget the goddamn money, will you?" he said. "Except what I spent buying the airfare back to Hawaii it's all there. Just take it."

She moved the belt away with her foot. "I'm sorry. I didn't mean that. The people here don't want money—nor do I. I want us to be friends."

"Okay." Brennan sat down, still looking annoyed.

A large elderly woman was walking toward them carrying two baskets. Martine went to greet her, taking the baskets and bringing them back with her to the fare.

"Lunch," she said. "Help yourselves—please."

The baskets contained freshly baked bread, marinated fish and sliced papaya. Carlisle took a hunk of bread and some fish, waiting for Martine to join them on the mat before he reopened the conversation. "Do you want to talk about things now?" he asked.

She nodded. "I don't know where to start, though."

He smiled at her. "That's easy. Soviet Typhoon-class submarines."

"I brought all my father's files here with me from Papeete," she said. "I can show you the press clippings from the Tahitian newspapers and ones from foreign papers, too."

"What do they say?" Carlisle asked.

"Only what I told Brennan on the phone. Mostly they're just reports of Russian submarine sightings in the South Pacific. There's a photograph of a submarine that the Americans took but it doesn't show anything very clearly. They did say it was definitely identified as a Soviet submarine."

"What else?" he prompted.

"Only that the Soviet Navy denied having any submarines anywhere near Mururoa. Apparently the Russians think the whole thing is silly." She hesitated. "The French are still making a huge fuss, though. Even in the last couple of weeks the TV and radio stations here have kept on saying how terrible it is to have Russian submarines in the waters round the atoll. I don't understand why the CEP get so excited. My father told me the Russians couldn't learn much about underground tests from a submarine anyway—even if it was very close to the atoll. Do you think that's right?"

"I don't know." Carlisle tried to imagine what instrumentation might be used. "I suppose they'd be able to pick up the size of the blast and see what levels of radioactive compounds there were in the sea and the air afterwards."

Brennan removed a piece of papaya skin from his mouth. "What do the Russians care?" he said. "They've got enough to worry about with the Americans without Moscow bothering to spy on a bunch of French tests all the way down here."

"There's nothing special about the type of bombs the French are testing, is there?" Carlisle asked.

Martine shook her head. "I don't think so. Anyway, there can't be a connection between submarines and what the French are calling their fallback position. Not when the French and the Russians don't even talk to each other about nuclear tests." She was sitting cross-legged on the mat in front of Zac, seemingly unaware of the way his eyes were straying beneath her skirt.

"There's a connection," Carlisle said. "Lefay mentioned both things in the same breath—not just once—lots of times."

"Mm." She self-consciously rearranged her legs. "We need someone inside the DGSE we can talk to."

From the remark Carlisle knew it was pointless even considering the possibility. "What about your people on the atoll?" he asked.

"This isn't something that's happening on the atoll. At least I don't think so. If it's some new system to seal the caverns the instructions will be coming from Paris. I've already asked Henri—he's the man who was with Brennan and Taufa at Giselle. He says the concreting program at Mururoa is still going on."

Brennan remembered Henri. "I didn't know he was working for your father," he said. "Henri's French."

She nodded. "I've told you before—you mustn't think it's only Tahitians who want to stop the testing."

"Okay, so what do we do?" Carlisle said. "Make a trip to Mururoa?"

"That's far too dangerous now." Martine took some bread from the basket. "The only idea I have is to ask someone in France to help us." She paused. "You know, see what we can find out by getting them to ask around in the right places."

"Do you know someone?" Carlisle asked.

"Not really. There's a man my father trusted. He's a journalist but he works for himself, I think. I've never met him."

"What the hell can he do?" Brennan went into the fare for his tobacco.

Martine smoothed down her skirt. "Have you and Brennan been friends for a long time?" she asked Carlisle.

"Zac used to work for me on the Big Island," he said. "We've known each other about eight or nine months."

"But you are friends?" She wanted an answer.

"Sure. We get on pretty well."

"Crap. He doesn't get on with anyone." Brennan was standing in the entrance rolling a cigarette with one hand. "He's an arrogant bastard. I've had him yelling his head off at me while I'm standing on a bed of hot lava trying to drill some stupid hole for him."

Martine smiled. "This is more difficult than drilling holes, isn't it?" she said. "I was hoping you'd have some kind of plan of what we ought to do."

"I don't want to decide on anything before I've had a look at your father's files," Carlisle said. "I don't mean I want to see them now—later on or tomorrow. I'm in the wrong mood for thinking at the moment."

She looked at her watch, then scrambled to her feet. "I'm sorry, I have to go. Is it all right if I leave you here and come back later?"

"Of course it is." Carlisle glanced up at her. "Don't worry about us."

"I'll try not to be too long." She hurried off along the beach.

"Did you mean that about not being in any mood to think?" Brennan said when she'd gone.

"No, but I figure you and I ought to do some talking by ourselves. That girl's gone to a lot of trouble and she expects us to be smarter than she is. I don't want to disappoint her."

"We haven't got a goddamn plan," Brennan said.

"By tomorrow we will have," Carlisle promised. "If we have to stay up all night we will have."

Despite his best intentions, Carlisle's estimate was to prove hopelessly optimistic. At dusk, after the fishing boats had returned to the village and the day's catch had been unloaded, a procession of adults and children began to approach the fare. Carrying torches, playing guitars and singing, they gathered outside, waiting patiently for their European visitors to appear.

Brennan emerged first, uncertain of what was expected of him. He called to Carlisle telling him to hurry.

Teenage girls were decorating Brennan with flower *heis* when Carlisle made his entrance. He bent down to accept his own heis of shells and red hibiscus flowers from another group of girls.

Martine came forward from the crowd to join them. "The people of my mother's village wish to welcome you," she said. "They've asked me to say they're honored to have you as their guests."

"Do I have to make a speech?" Carlisle whispered.

"No, no." She smiled. "Just say *maururu*—that's thank you. I'll do the rest. They're more embarrassed than you are."

After Carlisle had said thank you first in English and then in French and Tahitian there was a delay in the proceedings while Martine spoke to the villagers.

When she had finished he asked her what she'd said.

"I've told them you've come to help stop the testing on Mururoa but that no one must know you're here."

"Sounds as though you might have oversold us." Carlisle grinned.

"I said Brennan can fix the truck, too."

"Oh, thanks." Zac had adopted a five-year-old girl who was less shy than the other children. She was sitting on his knee, picking flowers from one of his heis for him to thread into her hair.

"You have to go to the party now," Martine explained. "The food's all laid out down on the beach. This is a very special evening for everyone."

For Carlisle, the evening was not only special, it was to mark the beginning of a remarkable experience. Over the next few days and nights, almost without realizing it, he slipped naturally into the rhythm of the village, enjoying every aspect of village life no matter how simple or how intriguing he found it to be and finding pleasure in the company of a people who had so readily accepted the presence of foreigners among them.

During the day, leaving Brennan to work on the truck assisted by an army of small children, Carlisle either reviewed Tumahai's files with Martine or spent his time alone on a part of the reef where the fishermen dried their nets while he grappled with the puzzle he was no closer to solving than he had been a week ago.

Not until the evening of their fourth day in the village did he make his decision. He walked from the fare to the store where Brennan was still busy with his welding torch.

Already the truck was a good deal more presentable. Using nothing more than steel cut from a plentiful supply of forty-gallon drums, Zac had fabricated door panels, fenders and a new roof for the cab.

Brennan switched off the torch as soon as he saw Carlisle. He removed his goggles and used a rag to wipe the sweat from his forehead.

"Do you want a swim?" Carlisle asked.

"Depends. Have you talked to Martine this afternoon?"

"No." Carlisle hadn't seen her all day.

"She heard a report on the radio at lunch time. Our friends in the Russian sub are back. This time a French reconnaisance plane got a real close look at it and took a bunch of photos. Apparently there's one hell of an uproar going on in Papeete and on Mururoa."

"Has there been anything from Moscow?" Carlisle, guessing the answer, climbed into the truck and sat behind the wheel.

"Same old thing—there's been a denial. Martine said the French aren't giving much away but the Russians are claiming they don't have any submarines in this part of the Pacific and even if they did have one here it wouldn't be a Typhoon-class type. Anyhow, it doesn't matter whether Moscow denies it or not, does it? Not if the French have got photos."

"It stinks," Carlisle said. "That's what I came to tell you. Martine's been translating those reports in the French newspapers for me—the early ones. They're all exaggerated—as though a Russian submarine popping up here is some kind of prelude to World War Three. The French are paranoid about it."

"So what? You thought that before."

"I know, but I wasn't as sure as I am now." Carlisle became more serious. "There's something else as well. At the back of one of Tumahai's files there's a clipping from a two-year-old magazine. I didn't ask Martine to translate it until yesterday. She'd seen it before but didn't think it was important."

"And you think it is?" Brennan was interested.

"I'm not certain yet. It's about a French schoolboy who lived in Cherbourg. He disappeared two days after he said he'd seen a huge submarine in the naval dockyard there. According to the article, his father got out a book from the library so they could identify what kind of submarine it was."

"And it was a Typhoon-class Russian sub," Brennan said caustically. "Surprise. You're not going to believe a yarn like that, are you?"

"Tumahai was interested enough to keep the clipping."

"What the hell would a Russian submarine be doing in a French dockyard?"

"No idea," Carlisle said. "Any more than I can figure out why the Soviets would bother to send one down here. They can't need data from the tests at Mururoa."

Brennan rolled a cigarette and lit it. "You're working up to something," he said. "I can tell."

"No, I'm not. I came to see what you think about getting Martine's journalist to sniff around in France for us."

"You mean Cherbourg, don't you?" Brennan grinned.

"And to see if he can find out why Soviet submarines at Mururoa are such a big deal to the French."

"Someone Tumahai trusted was funneling information to the DGSE. We don't know this journalist guy and Martine's never met him—she just said her father trusted him. That doesn't mean we should."

Carlisle jumped down from the cab. "I want to do it anyway. I've got a hunch Martine was right when she said the answer has to come from France."

"Can she get hold of him?"

"I haven't asked her yet."

Brennan stubbed out his cigarette and started stripping off his shirt. "You talk to her first. If you need me I'll be floating around in the lagoon for the next half hour."

"Okay." Carlisle went to find her.

She was sitting on a basket outside a fare owned by a large, well-dressed woman known universally to everyone in the village as Auntie Pau.

"Ah." Auntie Pau smiled broadly at him. "It is my friend who spends all day by himself on the reef. I have been practicing my English for you. It is good?"

"Perfect." Carlisle sat down on the ground.

"My son in London sends me more English-language tapes next month so I will soon learn Shakespeare." Auntie Pau stuck a finger into Carlisle's chest. "Your skin is darker like mine. The sun here is hotter than in Hawaii, I think."

"About the same," he said. "But I'm indoors most of the time in Hawaii."

"Is Brennan still working?" Martine inquired.

"No, he's gone swimming."

She frowned. "He went out too close to the pass yesterday. I've told him not to."

"Because of the sharks?"

"And the rip. It's a bad time for the tide right now."

In the past few days Carlisle had learned a great deal about Rangiroa and the Tiputa pass—a pass that linked the ocean with the largest lagoon in the largest coral atoll in the world. Rangiroa was also distinguished by its *motus,* the islands that formed a narrow ring inside the reef. Because these harbored an almost unbelievable assortment of marine life there were fish of every size and species swarming in the lagoon everywhere Carlisle had looked. And, as he knew very well, where fish were in such abundance, there would be sharks as well.

"Zac understands sharks," he said. "So do I."

Martine smiled slightly. "The sharks don't know that. Did you come to see me or are you visiting Auntie Pau?"

"Silly child," Auntie Pau snorted. She pulled her pareu around her and stood up. "You both go for a walk on the beach. I have to make supper."

"Sounds like an instruction." Carlisle grinned.

"I think it is." Martine accompanied him down to the water, listening while he explained what he wanted her to do.

"I can call France from the telephone at the airport or from the one at the Kia Ora Hotel," she said. "But I don't know if Vincent will be at the number I've got for him."

"Who?" Carlisle queried.

"Vincent. André Vincent—he's the journalist."

"How soon can you try?"

She thought for a second. "I was going to phone Papeete sometime tomorrow because Henri will be back there from Mururoa and we need to know what's happening on the atoll. I can make both calls tonight at the same time, I suppose."

"Do you think this Vincent guy will listen?"

"I don't know." Martine waded out into the lagoon, standing with her back to him. "He might believe we're asking him to go on a wild-goose chase. There can't have been a Russian submarine in Cherbourg." She turned around. "Can there?"

Carlisle didn't answer. Over the reef to the west the sun had vanished behind a bank of cloud, creating a soft orange glow across the lagoon. In front of him, illuminated by the glow, Martine stood with her skirt held halfway up her thighs with her skin on fire.

"Is something wrong?" she said.

"No." He dug his toes into the sand.

She waded back to him. "Brennan told me not to ask you anything about Stephanie," she said quietly.

"Zac doesn't understand." He smiled. "There's a lady called Eva who works for him in Hawaii. She's a bit like Auntie Pau. We had a long talk together before I left."

Martine waited for him to go on.

"Eva thought it was stupid for me to come here. She was wrong about that but right about everything else." He paused. "I don't mind talking about Steph—not now. I only knew her for a week—properly, I mean."

"You're really glad you came here?"

He nodded. "I didn't expect to find something like this anywhere here. Hawaii's very beautiful but it's not the same."

"That's what Brennan said. He likes it here too."

"It's you he likes. You be careful of Zac."

She compressed her lips as though irritated by his warning. "I'll go to the airport now, then—before it's too dark. The lights on the truck don't work."

"Okay."

"If I get through to André Vincent, I'll tell you later."

"Fine." Carlisle had been caught off balance by her change in mood.

She started to walk away. He called after her, "If Henri's there see if he knows how many caverns they've finished sealing on the atoll."

"All right." She answered without stopping.

Returning to the fare, he wondered whether there was more going on between Zac and Martine than he had originally thought and whether it mattered a damn one way or the other. In the end he decided the sunset and an overactive imagination had been playing tricks on him.

On the evening of their eighth day at the village the first breakthrough came. The information they had been waiting for—or at least what sounded something like it—arrived suddenly, as Carlisle had expected it would.

A few minutes ago Martine had returned from the airport after making her third long-distance phone call to André Vincent. Even before she climbed down from the truck it was clear she was the bearer of news. Her expression was animated and she was having difficulty in explaining what she had to say to them.

"Hey," Brennan said. "Slow down there."

"I'm sorry." She pulled her hair away from her face. "We'll have to get a windshield now you've made the truck go so much better."

"It needs brakes more than a windshield," Brennan said. "You're going to kill yourself in that thing, the way you drive."

"For Christ's sake," Carlisle interrupted. "Never mind

the truck. Vincent's been to Cherbourg and he's spoken to the boy's father—is that right?"

Martine nodded quickly. "Yes. André says there's absolutely no doubt what the boy saw. His father's certain and so are other people who worked in the dockyard—André's spoken to some of them, too. There were over fifty men who were employed on the project. They were issued with special security clearances from the French government before they started the job and the DGSE were there for the whole of the time."

"How the hell did Vincent get anyone to talk to him if it was a classified project?" Carlisle asked.

"Well, for a start, because it ended two years ago, lots of the men don't work at the dockyard anymore. The ones he saw don't believe the project was all that secret anyway—or they don't care. Vincent says most of them think the whole thing was a bit of a joke."

"But they must have known what they were working on," Carlisle said.

"Ah." She laughed. "They thought they did. The official story's really clever. The Cherbourg dockyard was asked to build a dummy superstructure of a big Russian nuclear submarine and fit it over the top of an old French submarine so NATO could operate it close to the Soviet coast in the North Atlantic. According to French naval experts, if the submarine was submerged it would give the same sonar echo as the genuine Russian model and, if the Russians ever saw it on the surface, they'd think it was one of theirs. Isn't that a neat story?"

Brennan was grinning. "Sounds pretty good to me. It might be true."

"That's what André originally thought," Martine said. "But he doesn't anymore. He agrees with John now. He spent a whole day going over all the newspaper reports of submarine sightings in the Pacific."

"And he thinks the French reports are hyped too?" Carlisle asked.

"Not just that. There are two other things. Apparently the French are flooding all the international press agencies with their new photos of the submarine off Mururoa and André says the earlier independent sightings by the Australian and U.S. navies could only have happened on purpose—because the French wanted them to see what they were supposed to think was a Russian submarine in the South Pacific."

"You mean the commander of a genuine Russian sub wouldn't have been stupid enough to surface when he knew he'd be seen?"

"That's right. And that's why the Russians have always denied having a Typhoon-class submarine anywhere near Mururoa." She spun around happily on one foot. "They've never had one here. John was right—it's all some sort of weird idea the French have dreamed up."

"It still doesn't make the slightest sense," Carlisle said. "Why in God's name would the CEP want to monitor their own tests at Mururoa in a fake Russian sub?"

"André doesn't know," she said. "But he wants to fly out. He's excited. He believes if he can get his own close-up photos of it he'll be able to force Paris into making a public statement."

"Good bloody luck," Brennan grunted. "If he's got some idea of winning an international prize for investigative journalism we'd better warn him. He doesn't know what he's up against."

"I've already explained that," Martine answered. "I said he couldn't come unless John thought it would be all right. I told him it might be dangerous."

"Are you supposed to call him back?" Carlisle was unhappy at the number of phone calls Martine had already made to France.

"Yes. Not straightaway, though." She misunderstood his

concern. "André wouldn't have gone to all this trouble and given me the information if he was working for the other side."

"I know that." Carlisle glanced at her. "You've phoned him three times now and you made that other call to Henri four days ago. Won't the people at the airport be wondering what's going on?"

"No." She shook her head. "Everyone around here uses the airport phone. Anyway, I made the call to Henri from the hotel."

"Henri went back to Mururoa yesterday," Brennan said. "It's a pity we didn't know about this before."

"We don't need Henri." Carlisle was deep in thought. "From what he said things have gone quiet there."

"Except that the CEP are still stopping people from swimming in the lagoon or anywhere outside the reef." Brennan lit a cigarette. "Henri told Martine there are signs up everywhere you look. I reckon the whole atoll's leaking like a goddamn sieve. I bet you a hundred bucks they've given up trying to fix it."

"Because they've decided to use their fallback solution instead," Carlisle said quietly. "They're going to use this Russian look-alike submarine of theirs. That's why it's here."

Some of Martine's exuberance was gone. She, too, was thinking. "It's crazy," she said. "How can the CEP stop the radioactivity leaking into the sea with a submarine?"

"They can't. It's just that we don't understand," Carlisle said. "I'm going to take a walk. I need time to sort this out."

"I'll go with you." Martine took her sunglasses from the truck.

"No. You and Zac see if you can figure out something by yourselves." Carlisle stuck his hands in his pockets and wandered off towards the reef.

When he returned to the fare much later in the evening, the village was in darkness. There was no sign either of Zac or Martine and, apart from the distant sound of waves breaking on the ocean side of the coral, it was very quiet.

He lay down on his mattress believing he was too preoccupied with the new twist in the puzzle to fall asleep. For a while his mind drifted away elsewhere and for a while he thought of Stephanie. Then Carlisle closed his eyes and stopped thinking altogether.

At dawn the next morning he was awoken by the sound of laughter. Two children—a boy and a girl—had sneaked into the fare. They were jumping up and down on Brennan's chest. He pretended to be still asleep. Just outside the entrance their father waited with an expression of acute embarrassment on his face.

"Gotcha." Brennan grabbed both the children at the same time. *"Ia ora na,"* he said. "I'll have the pair of you for breakfast."

Their father spoke in hesitant English. "Monsieur Brennan, we go for the asbestos which stops the wheels on the tractor," he said. "My boat she is ready for us now."

Carlisle propped himself up on an elbow, trying to make sense of the statement.

"Brake linings," Brennan explained. "Off an old tractor somewhere over on the other side of the lagoon. My friend here promised to take me today. If the stuff isn't too brittle I can use it on the truck."

"It'll only give Martine an excuse to drive faster," Carlisle said. "How long will you be?"

"Don't know. I'm supposed to be having some kind of picnic with these two tearaways when we get there." Brennan pulled the children down on top of him. "You haven't nutted anything out overnight, have you?"

"No. I will today, though." Carlisle chose to overlook the failure of his last prediction. "I'll have an answer by four o'clock."

The children scampered out of the fare the minute Brennan released them. "I'll find some fruit and get going," he said. "If there's a Russian sub anchored in the lagoon I'll come back and tell you."

The members of the brake-lining expedition were not the only early morning visitors to the fare. Barely ten minutes after Zac had gone, Martine arrived with Auntie Pau. Both women carried baskets covered in leaves.

"You are in serious trouble," Martine announced. "Auntie was expecting you for dinner last night."

"Oh, hell." He had forgotten. "I'm sorry. I got sidetracked."

"I cook you *tamaaraa* for seven hours." Auntie Pau looked at him sternly then burst into laughter. "You take it with you cold to the pass." She placed her basket carefully on the ground. "If you not like, the sharks can have it, but to be polite you must tell me you enjoy it very much."

"Thank you." Carlisle searched in vain for assistance from Martine.

"Have a nice day." Auntie Pau waved a hand and headed off towards the grocery store.

"What's going on?" Carlisle inquired. "What is tamaaraa and why do I have to take it somewhere?"

Martine smiled. "Tamaaraa is a way of cooking food in an underground pit full of hot rocks and leaves. She did a pig for you. It's a Tahitian holiday today. That's why the fishermen aren't working. I thought you'd like a trip to the pass so we can drift-snorkel through it when the tide changes."

"Through the pass?"

"Mm-hmm."

Carlisle frowned at her. "I seem to remember you telling me the Tiputa pass is one of the most treacherous, shark-infested places in the world."

"It is."

"Then why are we going there to drift-snorkel?"

"You'll see. It's safe if you know what you're doing. I've already borrowed a boat."

Although he was anxious not to disappoint her, he was unwilling to spend a day at the pass when there was work to do.

"We can talk about the submarine when we get there." She had sensed his reluctance. "Come on. All you need are swimming things. I've got everything else and Auntie Pau has made us lunch."

The size of the borrowed boat did little to reassure him. It was less than twelve feet long, and even though the hull appeared to be sound and the outboard motor was obviously new, Carlisle decided that it was hardly suitable for the trip Martine had in mind.

The newness of the motor did not surprise him. By now, he had been long enough in the village to appreciate that the simple life led by the fishermen and their families had nothing to do with the Paumoto people being poor or unsophisticated. Wherever technology could contribute to any easier way of making a living the villagers used it—even if their treatment of machinery drove Zac to despair.

Once Martine had started the outboard, Carlisle shoved the bow of the boat off the beach and climbed in.

"The pass is just round the corner along the reef," Martine said. She was sitting in the stern with both hands on the tiller and seemed in particularly good spirits. "We've left a bit late, I think."

With the village behind them, on the starboard side the coral rose almost vertically from the lagoon, telling Carlisle they must be nearing the pass. Already he could see white water curving past the point ahead of them. He trailed a hand over the side, enjoying his first trip away from the village since his arrival on Rangiroa.

Martine throttled back the motor and stood up to look. "Get ready with that rope," she instructed. "There won't be much time because of the rip."

Rounding the point, the boat suddenly picked up speed. Before them was the pass—a three-hundred-foot-wide channel in the coral filled with an avalanche of surging water.

"Go," she shouted.

Grabbing the rope, Carlisle sprang onto an overhanging rock, hauling the bow of the boat into a cleft in the coral on the seaward side. He fought to hold on until Martine clambered forward to help pull the boat up onto a miniature beach of coarse white sand.

"Thanks for the advance warning," Carlisle panted. "What happens if you miss the beach?"

"You end up half a kilometer out to sea and have to wait for the tide to change before you come back in." She was laughing. "Isn't it great?" Her face was wet with spray and her eyes were sparkling.

"We aren't snorkeling out there, are we?" Carlisle asked.

"Not yet. As soon as the tide changes we'll go outside the reef in the boat. When the water starts moving back into the lagoon we drift in with it." She stripped off her pareu. Beneath it she wore a bikini. It was a pale blue and seemed to exaggerate the color of her skin and the tautness of her body.

Because Carlisle hadn't seen her dressed like this before, he became uncomfortably aware of her desirability and of his reaction to her figure. For a second he imagined her with Zac on the soft, warm nights in the village when they had disappeared along the beach together.

"Okay," she said. "Breakfast. Then we sunbathe and we can talk if you want to." She started unloading the boat, passing him the food, masks and spear guns to carry up the beach. They made their camp there on two towels, Martine stretching out on one, waiting for him to begin the conversation.

Knowing she was being careful not to press him and conscious of circumstances that he thought were somehow inappropriate, it took him nearly two hours to unwind. But once he had, it was not difficult for Carlisle to decide he might never discuss the problems of Mururoa atoll again.

Here, on the very edge of Rangiroa's gigantic emerald lagoon with the roar of the sea coursing through the pass, the world was a different place—a world where there was no need for nuclear warheads, for submarines or for men who would kill to protect the secrets of their governments. And, as the day wore on and the rush of water through the pass began to slacken, lying motionless on his towel, there came a new awakening inside himself. The waters of the Tiputa pass were the catharsis by which the past could be accepted if it could not be forgotten, and the change in his life was a change not to be resisted but to be met head on.

Eyes shut against the sun, for the first time he allowed himself to think of a fresh and unknown future.

At four o'clock Martine announced that they should begin to get ready. Already the pass was quite unlike the stretch of water it had been earlier. Instead of the eddies and whirlpools that had been swirling past the cleft this morning when the tide had been going out, now, from one side of the pass to the other, the water was flat and only just starting to move back into the lagoon.

With the outboard on half throttle they headed out against the current between cliffs of jagged rock until they had completely cleared the reef and were some way out to sea.

She handed him a mask, snorkel and flippers. "It doesn't take long for the rip to get going," she said. "You'd better make sure those fit you properly."

"What about the boat?"

"We let it drift on ahead of us. We each hold a rope tied onto the stern so we don't get left behind or lose each other."

"Do we take the spear guns?"

"No." She shook her head. "I only brought them in case you wanted to do some fishing in the lagoon."

She had planned the day carefully, Carlisle thought. "I don't need flippers," he said. "I'm used to pretty strong rips in Hawaii."

"The soles of your feet are white. The minute you start kicking you'll attract the sharks."

Without further argument he put on the flippers, then slipped the mask over his face.

"Here." Martine gave him a rope. "Don't let go." She prepared to abandon ship.

Gripping the rope firmly in his right hand he followed her backward over the side.

And there, eighty feet below him, was a seascape of truly breathtaking color—coral heads, pink sand, cliffs that seemed to dissolve as he swept over them and an unbelievable array of fish.

The rip was tugging at him now, carrying him faster and faster into the mouth of the pass itself. Shoals of trumpet fish, wrasse, yellow butterfly fish and silver jacks were making the ride as well, pouring through the gap at different depths. He saw a huge grouper and watched surgeon fish with their razor-sharp fins darting among multicolored damselfish as though they were playing some kind of game.

Beside him, kicking with her flippers to bring her closer, Martine reached out to hold his hand. She pointed downwards to a pair of black-tipped sharks. They were traveling together at a depth of about thirty feet, unconcerned at the presence of the two observers on the surface.

The panorama continued to unfold—a dizzying, three-dimensional film of Rangiroa's secret place—a five-hundred-yard ride through the pass into the more tranquil waters of the lagoon.

As soon as they were out of the main current, Martine began pulling on her rope, bringing the boat towards them.

Carlisle hauled himself over the side, then helped Martine climb aboard.

She removed her mask. "Well?"

"Tremendous, absolutely tremendous." He had never experienced anything like it. "Can we do it again?"

She was doubtful. "The rip can get up to over fifteen knots once the tide really starts to run. I think we'd better come back another day."

"Okay."

"We can spear fish, though. In the lagoon." She hadn't expected him to be this pleased.

"No, that'd spoil it." He smiled at her. "*Mauruuru roa* for bringing me."

She laughed at his pronunciation. "You're welcome. I'm glad you enjoyed it. Are you sure you don't want to take some fish back for supper?"

"No, let's go home and see if Zac's there yet," he said. "I want to tell him what he's missed."

"All right." Concealing her disappointment she started the outboard and swung the bow of the boat towards home.

They were four or five hundred yards from the village, approaching the southeast end of the beach when Carlisle saw the launch.

He scrambled quickly across the seat, cut the motor and rammed the tiller to one side.

"What are you doing?" He'd frightened Martine.

"Grab an oar," Carlisle instructed. "We've got visitors. Paddle over to the shore. Do what I say—quickly."

By now Martine had seen the launch. It was floating at anchor near one of the fishing boats a short way off the beach. Paddling quietly, they edged the boat closer to a rocky shelf where some fishing nets were drying.

Carlisle slipped over the side into waist-deep water, towing the boat behind him to the shelf. "Throw me the rope," he said.

She jumped out and helped him lash it round a palm stump. "Who is it?" she whispered.

"I don't know, but I don't like the look of it. That's a big seagoing launch and there's a bloody great radar dish on the bridge." He stopped talking suddenly, imagining he'd heard a scream. "We'll crawl up through the bush and see what's going on."

Martine had already put on her shoes and was starting to climb the coral.

"Hang on." He went back to the boat to collect the spear guns. "Here." He handed her one. "Don't make any noise."

"No one knows you're at the village," Martine whispered.

"You want to bet?" Carlisle was worried. If Zac had returned early, the arrival of the launch was certain to have caught him unawares.

Keeping well hidden in the vegetation bordering the eastern boundary of the village they made their way to a gap between some trees where the reef overlooked the plateau.

Laid out in front of him on the beach was the very scene Carlisle had dreaded most.

Two men wearing combat fatigues were holding submachine guns on a group of terrified villagers while a third man was fondling a naked teenage girl. She was entangled helplessly in a fishing net and screaming.

Carlisle recognized the man at once.

It was Lobrutto.

EIGHT

CROUCHED in the scrub with his heart pounding, Carlisle switched his attention to the launch. If the three men on the beach were alone, there was a slim chance of taking them by surprise, but if more men were on the bridge or belowdecks, any sort of rescue operation was out of the question.

The girl in the fishing net had stopped screaming. Lobrutto had left her tied up outside the store and was standing with his hands on his hips shouting at the villagers in French.

"What's going on?" Carlisle whispered.

"He's asked them if they've seen two Europeans anywhere on Rangiroa. They've said they haven't but he doesn't believe them." Martine's face was pale and she was biting her lip. "That man's from the DGSE, isn't he?"

Carlisle nodded. "He works for Lefay."

"What are we going to do?"

"Depends how many of them there are." There was still no sign of any movement on the launch but Carlisle needed to be sure.

Lobrutto had begun shoving one of the fishermen in the chest.

"They can't be certain you've been here," Martine whispered. "He's asking how to get to other villages on the island."

Carlisle breathed a little easier. If the DGSE were guessing, the three men on the beach could be the total number in the party. The odds were hardly in their favor but they were improving—especially as Zac had evidently not yet returned, which meant he was still somewhere out in the lagoon and could arrive to help at any time. Except that the launch would be warning enough to prevent him from coming ashore, Carlisle thought, provided he arrived in daylight and saw it before the men on the beach saw him.

In front of the store Lobrutto was pacing up and down, shouting again.

"He's threatening to rape the girl," Martine said. "He's saying that by keeping quiet the villagers are admitting they know something. We can't just stay here and watch. The girl will tell him even if her parents don't."

"We're not staying here." There was a coldness inside Carlisle and a feeling of extraordinary calm. "It won't matter what she tells him." He looked at her. "Can we get to the track from here?"

"Yes."

"How long will it take?"

"A few minutes." She had seen his expression harden. "John, we can't let that man rape the girl."

"We haven't got a choice," Carlisle said quietly. "There are two of us against three armed men. And we can't afford to wait for Zac. Load your spear gun and show me the way to the track."

She hesitated.

"Do it," he instructed.

Sitting down, Martine put her feet into the stirrup at the nose of the gun and pulled back on the rubber straps with both hands until the bolt clicked. She loaded the spear without saying anything.

When he had checked that her safety catch was on he loaded his own gun. "Okay," he said. "I'll follow you."

It took them just over five minutes to reach the big outcrop of rock where the track opened out onto the plateau. Bleeding from scratches all over her, Martine had lost one of her shoes and she was out of breath. Equally breathless, Carlisle was in better shape except for a grazed knee and a gash in his cheek from an encounter with a thorn bush. He'd been wearing a shirt when they'd left the pass, which, despite being badly ripped, had offered some protection during their long uphill crawl through the scrub.

Propping his gun against the rock, he wiped the sweat out of his eyes. Ahead of them on a treeless expanse of sand stood the village store. Guarding each side of the front door armed men were leaning against the building talking. One of them began to laugh.

"You'll have to help me," Carlisle said. "I can't do this by myself."

"I know."

"We duck back through the bush until we're facing the rear wall of the store," he said, "so we're right behind it. Then we walk out into the open. As long as those guys stay where they are they won't be able to see us."

She nodded.

"When we reach the back wall, you go around one side, I go around the other."

She nodded again.

"And when you hear me shout, you use your spear gun." He kept his voice level.

This time she did not respond.

"Martine?" he queried.

"What about the other man?" she whispered.

"He's inside with the girl. Leave him to me." He picked up his spear gun. "Are you ready?"

"Just a second." She pulled back her hair and tied it in a knot behind her head.

Carlisle glanced at the launch for the last time, no longer concerned whether there were other men on board or not. Gradually the coldness had taken over. Instead of fear there was a detachment from reality, a calm, unemotional acceptance of what he had to do. Beside him Martine was clearly nervous. She was still breathing fast and both her hands were shaking.

"There isn't another way," Carlisle said gently.

"Don't talk to me." She kept her eyes on the ground.

"Okay. Make sure your safety catch is off and stay behind me." Reentering the scrub he headed for a tree on the outskirts of the plateau. When they reached it, the store obscured their view of the men and of the villagers they were guarding. Slowly Carlisle emerged from the cover. Then he began to walk, concentrating all his attention on the store.

They were in full view of the launch now with no protection and no hope of retreating if there was someone on board who saw them. At the halfway point, a hundred feet from the building, he turned around, motioning for Martine to walk beside him. She was limping and she had bitten through her lip.

Wiping away the blood with his finger, he took her hand, not releasing it until they reached the rear wall. So far they had been undetected. Now comes the tough bit, Carlisle thought. He pointed to his left. "Off you go," he whispered. "Quietly as you can."

She glanced at him before vanishing silently around the corner.

Keeping close to the right-hand wall of the store, gripping his spear gun in both hands, Carlisle began inching forward.

The villagers had seen them now. Twenty or thirty people grouped near the truck only a few feet away. One of the women started to point.

"Go," Carlisle yelled.

Rounding the corner he came face to face with the guards. Both began to raise their weapons. Instinctively, Carlisle squeezed the trigger on his gun, seeing the man nearest to him clutch the spear that had pierced his chest before he coughed and collapsed sideways against the building.

Shouting the alarm, unaware of Martine's presence behind him the other guard had his gun leveled. For a second he sensed Carlisle's helplessness and for a second he hesitated.

The delay was fatal. Martine's spear entered beneath his arm, nailing him to the corrugated iron wall. He died at once, his gun unfired.

"Get back," Carlisle yelled at her.

She was retreating when the front door burst open. Through it came the girl, naked, running like a rabbit down the beach toward people who seemed too stunned to help her.

Before she could reach them Lobrutto appeared in the doorway. With one hand he was pulling up his trousers, in the other he held an automatic.

Carlisle saw him pull the trigger and, as if in slow motion, saw the bullet hole appear in the girl's back between her shoulders.

She fell heavily, first to her knees, then slowly toppling face down unmoving on the sand.

For the Frenchman there was no second chance. Before he could move, the butt of Carlisle's spear gun slammed into his neck, unbalancing him.

Martine was struggling to reload her spear gun when Carlisle saw her. "No," he shouted. "Leave him. I've got the bastard." He wrenched at the Frenchman's arm, using all his strength to ram him headlong into the corrugated iron.

Several fishermen arrived to help. One retrieved Lobrutto's gun from the ground while others seized him and started battering his head repeatedly against the wall.

"Make them stop," Carlisle shouted. "They'll kill him."

Martine intervened, telling them to hold the Frenchman until someone could fetch a rope.

Lobrutto had lost a tooth and his nose was bleeding but he was far from dead. He spat a mouthful of blood at Carlisle. "You make a bad mistake, Englishman," he said. "If I not return, tomorrow the DGSE come to find me."

Carlisle studied him dispassionately. "You've just raped and killed a girl from this village," he said. "I wouldn't worry too much about tomorrow if I were you. The people here might want to level things up."

Lobrutto struggled while his wrists and ankles were tied, but he made no further mention of the DGSE or of a search party.

To his surprise, Carlisle felt nothing—no satisfaction in capturing one of the men who had killed Stephanie, no relief that the raid was over and no revulsion at the violence. The coldness was all-pervading, controlling how he thought and everything he did.

"Where's Lefay?" he said.

"Papeete. He find you soon and this pretty bitch, I think." Lobrutto looked at Martine. Her bikini was spattered in blood and she was trembling. "You have killed two men and this is French territory. From here you cannot escape. You are finished."

Turning his back on him, Carlisle began leading Martine away. He pried the spear gun loose from her fingers, dropping it on the ground behind him.

Auntie Pau had come to meet them. Tears were rolling down her cheeks. She enveloped Martine in her arms, taking her from him.

"Is the girl dead?" He knew the question was unnecessary.

Auntie Pau nodded. "She has died in front of her

mother. It is not good for a mother to see such a thing, I think. These men who come to our village are worse than animals. I promise that the one who lives will pay for what he does here today. We use the old ways."

Martine freed herself. "No," she said. "Don't let the men do anything to him. Let John decide, please."

Auntie Pau frowned at Carlisle. "You have brought suffering to our village. Is this how you will stop the testing at Mururoa?"

He had no answer for her. There was no answer—no means of justifying the death of a girl in front of her own mother. Just as events had overtaken him in Hawaii, what had happened here had been unforeseen and equally terrible—a repeat of the horror of the fire at Wailuku, except that this time the girl had been a stranger. And this time, Carlisle thought, the situation had worsened to the point where a whole village might now be threatened.

"I take Martine with me," Auntie Pau said. "Then I arrange for the girl's body to be removed." She waved toward the lagoon. "Your friend Brennan is back. When you have spoken with him and decided what is to be done with the dead men you come to see me. I will need to know how you will explain this to the French authorities."

At the water's edge the returning fishing boat was tying up alongside the launch. Zac was standing in the bow shouting. He jumped overboard, waded ashore and walked slowly up the beach looking at the bodies.

"Jesus bloody Christ." Brennan's face was grim. "What the hell happened?"

Carlisle told him.

"You and Martine?" Brennan was incredulous. He watched some women carry away the body of the girl.

"If you mean did we manage to get that girl killed—yes we did." Carlisle corrected himself. "I did." The coldness was wearing off.

"Where's Lobrutto?"

"Tied up in the store. The villagers have got him." Carlisle paused. "There was no reason for him to shoot the girl. Auntie Pau's right."

"About what?"

"She thinks men like Lobrutto are worse than animals." Carlisle glanced at the store. "Martine had to stop the fishermen from killing the bastard. I don't know how long he'll last in there with them."

"Who cares." Brennan had detected the flatness in the way Carlisle was speaking. "Is Martine okay?"

"Pretty shaken. I'm more worried about Lobrutto."

"Because we need him?"

"Right now he's all we've got."

Brennan sat down and began throwing stones into the lagoon. "It's not going to take the DGSE long to start wondering what's happened to three of their men. They're going to come looking for their launch, too."

"That's what Lobrutto said. I think we can fix things, though. Martine took me out to the pass today."

The connection between the launch and Carlisle's visit to the pass was not obvious to Brennan. He waited for Carlisle to explain.

"As long as we can get some help and as long as you can use a radio transmitter we can insulate the village." Carlisle sat down beside him. "There's a radar on the launch, so it's bound to have a decent radio, don't you think?"

"Sure. Who are we going to radio—the U.S. Navy or the cavalry?"

"The French. The DGSE or the CEP—anyone who's listening. It doesn't matter who."

Brennan was no further ahead. "Okay, let's have it," he said. "What's the deal?"

"You take half a dozen men on board the launch and hack off anything that isn't needed to make it float. Stack all the bits where we can get at them—life rafts, seats, bits of the bridge—whatever you can find."

"But not the radio." Brennan smiled slightly. "Or the engine."

"Anything that'll float to make it look as though the thing's hit a rock on its way out of the lagoon. From what I've seen of the pass it's real easy to get into trouble there."

"Why not scuttle the whole launch?"

"Maybe we can use it. I don't know what for yet but it looks pretty handy."

"So we're going to let the French think they've lost a launch in the pass." Brennan considered the idea. "Suppose Lobrutto already radioed to say he was at the village?"

"We're not leaving until tonight. The French will figure the launch went down on its way home." Carlisle thought for a moment. "We can say so when we radio the distress calls."

"So we'll need someone who can speak French," Brennan said. "Properly, I mean."

"And someone who can navigate us out through the pass and back. I don't think Martine can handle the launch."

"I'll go and rustle up a crew." Brennan stood up and stretched. "I'll see if Martine will ask the fishermen to give me a hand."

"No." Carlisle shook his head. "Auntie Pau's calling the shots. And you haven't heard it all yet."

Although his friend's voice was not yet normal, Brennan sensed he had at least recovered from the immediate effects of the raid. He sat down again, brushed the sand from his fingers and began rolling a cigarette.

"I want Lobrutto and the bodies of the guards on board the launch and we'll need a fishing boat to follow us." Carlisle started speaking more quietly, explaining what he had in mind while Brennan listened with increasing interest.

An hour and a half later in front of a different audience Carlisle's proposal was met with less enthusiasm.

"No." Auntie Pau shook her head firmly. "It is not necessary. There is no need to wait for information from the Frenchman. He remains here. I will get what you want before you leave for the pass."

"How?"

"You do not need to know."

"I do," Carlisle said. "Lobrutto knows what's going on at Mururoa. I have to talk to him myself."

"Give me your questions." Auntie Pau looked at Carlisle. "I get the answers for you."

"Not unless you tell me how."

Auntie Pau sighed. "The children will take a jar to catch the scorpions which live under the palm trees by the big rocks. They get ten, maybe twenty. Then we take the clothes off this man, tie him to the ground and tell him we will fix the scorpions to him with threads of flax. You understand?"

Carlisle understood very clearly. "What happens after he's answered the questions?"

Auntie Pau's face was impassive. "When you go to the pass you take his body with the others."

A month ago Carlisle would have recoiled from the idea. Now, here on Rangiroa, after all that had gone before, he was shocked to find he could consider it.

"No," he said. "The Frenchman comes with us."

"Later you bring him back here?"

Carlisle shook his head. "Once the French know the launch is missing they're going to be all over the village asking questions. We don't want Lobrutto anywhere near here."

"It is simpler to kill him than to hide him. You saw him murder the child and I know what he has done in Hawaii."

"Who told you about Hawaii?"

"Three days ago, Zac tells me all of it." Auntie Pau stared at him. "The Frenchman does not deserve to live."

"There are a couple of others who don't deserve to live

either," Carlisle grunted. "But I'm not letting you kill Lobrutto with scorpions. I want him on the launch—alive."

Auntie Pau frowned. "You go tonight?"

"Yes." Carlisle hesitated. "Zac and I can't do this by ourselves."

"All this is necessary to stop the testing at Mururoa and to protect the people of my village?"

"I wouldn't be asking for your help if I didn't think so." He evaded the question. "I'm doing what I think's best."

"Then I will talk to the elders and tell Martine she is to go with you." Auntie Pau reached out to place a hand on Carlisle's shoulder. "Also, I pray for you."

"Thank you." He was embarrassed. "I'm truly sorry for what's happened. It was wrong for Zac and me to have come here."

"Perhaps." Auntie Pau's expression softened. "But I think it is no longer possible for my people to pretend that the world outside does not exist. For a generation we have ignored what is going on at Mururoa. Now, because the struggle against the French has been brought to the shores of our village and because of what Martine has explained about the radioactivity, maybe this is the time for us to fight for our future instead of allowing strangers to do it for us."

She removed her hand. "We will help you, John Carlisle," she said. "But you must understand it will be in our own way. Go now to help your friend Brennan prepare the launch."

Carlisle left feeling unsettled. The qualification in her parting remark had been undisguised, but because he had no way of knowing what she meant he gave it no further thought until evening when they were already on board the launch making ready to depart.

By then, as a result of several hours' energetic work by Brennan and his helpers, the launch was a floating wreck. Lashed in place by ropes, parts of the bridge were hanging over the side; the almost totally destroyed life raft was piled in a heap at the bow and even nonstructural sections of the hull had been stripped out and smashed ready to be dropped overboard when they reached the pass.

"What do you think?" Zac was pleased with himself.

"Looks pretty good." Carlisle inspected some of the damaged pieces. "I suppose it depends on whether anyone bothers to collect the bits. You can see ax marks on some of them."

"You know they're ax marks. The French won't."

"Yeah." Carlisle was not convinced. "Let's hope so."

"We found two more guns on board and half a dozen bottles of whiskey. That means we've got four machine guns altogether as well as Lobrutto's automatic."

"What've you done with the whiskey?"

"Tipped it over the side." Brennan grinned. "Well, most of it. We've given the empty bottles to Auntie Pau. She's going to claim the crew were half drunk when they got here." He paused. "Assuming someone asks her."

"They will," Carlisle assured him. "What about the radio?"

"Piece of cake but I need some more time if you want me to drive the radar." Brennan pointed. "Here's Martine with our friend from the DGSE."

Dressed in a fresh blue pareu, Martine stood at the bow of a small fishing boat that was drawing alongside. She spoke briefly to a group of men holding Lobrutto before stepping onto the deck of the launch.

"Are we ready to go?" Her voice was brittle.

This was their first meeting since the raid and in the dusk Carlisle couldn't see her face properly. "Yes," he said. "Are you okay?"

"Why shouldn't I be?" She avoided his eyes. "Four men are coming on the launch with us and the others will follow in the boat."

"Why four?"

"One to speak French over the radio, one to handle the

launch for us when we get to the pass, and the other two are looking after the Frenchman. Does it matter how many there are?"

"No, I guess not. Let's get everyone on board."

Martine called to the men on the fishing boat, introducing each of them as they clambered over the rail onto the launch.

"Do you think this'll work?" she asked Carlisle.

"Has Auntie Pau told you what we're going to do?"

She nodded. "Suppose Lobrutto won't talk?"

"He'll have to. This is probably the only chance we'll get to find out what the hell the French are really up to. Lobrutto works for the DGSE. Don't forget that. He knows damn well what the submarine's for."

"Mm." She glanced quickly at him. "I'm sorry about this afternoon—about leaving you alone, I mean. Auntie Pau wouldn't let me come and talk to you. She wanted to talk about my father and what he'd been trying to do."

"It's okay." Carlisle watched Lobrutto being manhandled onto the launch. The Frenchman was bound and gagged but surprisingly seemed to be in one piece. Two fishermen tied him to the rail near some large plastic buckets while the other two crew members went to join Brennan on what remained of the bridge.

Carlisle was on the point of asking what the buckets were for when there was a roar from the engines. Zac shouted for the anchor to be winched up.

"Hang on," Carlisle yelled. "Where's the rope?"

"It's here." Martine kicked at a coil lying on the deck beside the bodies of the dead guards. "We've got to get going. I asked Zac to hurry because of the tide. Even in a boat this big we don't want to be out in the pass at the height of the rip."

The launch was underway, already leaving the fishing boat behind.

"Do those guys know they can stay inside the lagoon?" Carlisle asked.

"Yes. I said we wouldn't be very long. They'll wait for us."

"Okay. I have to go and talk to Zac," he said. "About what we do afterwards."

"I'll stay here." She searched his face for a moment.

Carlisle left her at the rail and went to join Brennan on the bridge. He stood there for a while watching the few lights in the village slip away into the darkness as the moon rose clear of the reef to disappear behind a thin wisp of cloud that had drifted across its face.

"Are you sure you can hide this damn thing?" Carlisle asked.

"Not a problem." Brennan opened the throttles wider. "Some of the *motus* I saw today have inlets big enough to swallow a couple of boats this size. A lot of them are overgrown, too. Soon as we've chucked this stuff over the side and had our little chat with Monsieur Lobrutto I'll head straight off. By morning no one's ever going to know we've got this baby hidden anywhere on Rangiroa atoll."

"What about Lobrutto? Do you want one of the fishermen to go with you?"

Brennan smiled. "I can handle him. There's a real nice locker to tie him up in belowdecks. It stinks of diesel and it'll be hot as hell. He'll be fine in there."

Carlisle wondered if Zac had heard about the scorpions. "Now listen," he said. "Wherever you hide the launch you stay there until one of the fishing boats comes looking for you. I'll arrange for the boat to fly something green from its mast. If you see a boat that doesn't have a green flag, keep quiet and keep your head down."

"While I've got my head down what are you going to be doing?"

"Depends what Lobrutto has to tell us. Martine and I will have to camp out someplace until we're sure it's safe to go back to the village. We'll decide after that. I don't think there's anything else we can do right now."

"What about letting this guy Vincent fly out from Europe? He wants to come and he could be here in a couple of days. We're kind of shorthanded, aren't we?"

"Maybe." Carlisle didn't want to be rushed.

Ahead, sparkling in the moonlight, he could see flecks of white water at the mouth of the pass. He went to find Martine so she could alert the fisherman who would guide the launch through the gap in the coral. She had moved to the bow where she was standing alone with one hand on the rail and the other holding her hair away from her face.

"Hi." He braced himself against the rail. "It's time. The minute we hit the rough water I want to start transmitting the distress calls on the radio."

"I don't see why we have to send the signals from the pass," she said. "Why can't we do it afterwards from inside the lagoon when we have more time?"

"Because that's too easy. There's a chance the French'll pick us up on more than one receiver. If they're quick and they hear us at three different locations they'll be able to calculate the position of our transmitter. I want them to be sure our signals are coming from where we say they're coming from."

"Oh." She smiled tightly at him. "I'll go and help on the bridge then—while you and Zac talk to Lobrutto. Good luck."

The launch was just beginning to enter the pass now, lurching heavily in the swell and gaining speed as the rip took hold.

Struggling to keep his balance he made his way aft to where Zac was already waiting.

"This is it," Carlisle said. He cupped his hands, shouting up to Martine against the wind. "Tell the radio guy to start transmitting and make sure he keeps repeating our position at the Tiputa pass."

One at a time he rolled the bodies of the guards over the side, then began cutting free the wreckage. Beside him, Zac was already hurling pieces of timber into the water.

"The fishermen are going to send up some flares," Brennan said. "It was their idea. They reckon there's a good chance the French'll see them from one of the naval ships."

He had barely finished speaking when the first flare exploded skyward. For a second, in the light bouncing off the cliffs, there was a glimpse of flotsam surrounding the launch, some of it already lodged against the coral.

For no good reason, with each flare Carlisle found himself looking for the beach where he'd spent the morning with Martine. But at night the pass was a different place—a wild, unrecognizable place he had only seen in brilliant sunshine in a very different frame of mind. Even if he could have picked out the beach, recalling the few hours of pleasure spent there with a girl who was unconscious of her effect on him was as futile as it was stupid, he thought. Particularly at a time like this.

"All done." Brennan jettisoned the last pieces of the life raft as the final flare went up. "Let's find out why the hell we're doing all this." He released Lobrutto from the rail, yanked him to his feet and cut the gag away from his mouth.

The Frenchman's eyes were sullen. "You are not so clever," he said. "By morning the wreckage will be out in the ocean."

"That's right." Carlisle pushed Lobrutto's head over the side. "Have a good look. Think what it'd be like to be out there with it. We're going to tow you behind the launch at the end of a rope but we can cut you loose any time we feel like it. Have you got the idea?"

Lobrutto remained silent.

"If you want to stay on board and avoid the sharks all you have to do is talk," Carlisle said. "Explain how this clever submarine of yours is going to clean up the mess at Mururoa. It's a nice easy question and all I need is a nice easy answer."

"There are sharks here?" Fear showed in Lobrutto's eyes.

Carlisle became less confident. The Frenchman's ignorance of the shark hazard was a disadvantage.

"Ask the fishermen," Carlisle said. "Now are you going over the side or not?"

Almost before Lobrutto could reply, two of the villagers had looped the free end of the rope around the Frenchman's wrists and had him halfway over the rail.

"Wait," Carlisle said. "Give the bastard a chance. What about it, Lobrutto?"

When there was no response, the men acted.

"Jesus." Brennan watched the rope uncoiling until it went taut. "He's mad."

"Maybe." Carlisle was looking for fins. "I don't think he's in much danger. Not if we don't leave him too long."

"How long?"

"I don't know. We'll be outside the pass in a few minutes." Carlisle nodded at the fishermen, who started to reel Lobrutto in. They pulled him gasping over the side and dumped him unceremoniously on the deck.

Lobrutto vomited seawater. "If I tell you—you not put me in there again."

"Let's hear it," Brennan said coldly.

The Frenchman fought for breath.

"Martine." Carlisle called to her. "Cut back on the speed and keep us steady against the current."

"Come on." Brennan prodded Lobrutto with his foot.

"I speak." He sat up. "First it is necessary to understand that the caverns where there have been explosions at Mururoa are high in radioactivity and that the sea is leaking into these caverns. Because the clay layer is now no good after so many tests, the radioactive water is moving from the caverns up into the lagoon. From the lagoon it already flows into the ocean."

"Yeah, yeah," Brennan said. "We know all that. What about the goddamn submarine?"

"It takes too much money to concrete all of the caverns so we must do something else."

"The sub," Brennan prompted. "The sub."

"I am telling you. We take a French submarine upon which we build a big pretend Russian submarine—just the top of it. Then we make sure many times that this submarine is seen to be spying at Mururoa." Lobrutto coughed. "Soon we make a big fire on board so it must surface near the atoll for the television cameras. Many people will see it all over the world."

Carlisle caught his breath. This was the French fall-back—the answer to the puzzle. He controlled his impatience, waiting for the punch line.

"You give me a cigarette," Lobrutto said.

"Piss off." Brennan prodded him again. "Think of the sharks."

"Still for television we tow the burning submarine into the Mururoa lagoon to stop it from sinking in deep water but you understand our efforts are not enough and we fail, so the submarine sinks in the lagoon. Afterwards we say the nuclear reactor is broken and it is not possible to stop much radioactivity from leaking into the water."

"Oh my God!" Martine had come down from the bridge in time to hear. "You're going to blame the radioactivity on the submarine—on the Russians."

Carlisle was silent, thinking, marveling at a plan of such simplicity and of such enormous daring. Though they would be seen to be unsuccessful the French would be hailed as heroes, risking lives in attempting to prevent an international disaster of horrendous proportions. And after Chernobyl, with the Soviet Union in political and economic chaos, what could the Russians do? How could they explain away what would seem to be conclusive evidence of their crippled submarine burning and sinking in

French territorial waters? The French fallback position was just that—a strategy to blame another country, a cheap solution to cover up the poisoning of the South Pacific because the French could no longer afford either to prevent it or to control it.

Brennan was strangely quiet. Now, when he spoke, it was to echo Carlisle's own thoughts. "Christ," he said. "And we never picked it—never even got close. It's perfect. Soviet subs have been catching fire all over the place in the last two years. People are just going to believe this is another one. After Chernobyl no one trusts the Russians. What a hell of an idea."

"Now you give me cigarette." Lobrutto was insistent.

"You're not getting anything," Carlisle grunted. "Just shut up."

Absorbed in thought he only half heard one of the fishermen say something in Tahitian.

"What did he say?" Carlisle asked.

"He wants to know if you have any more questions." Martine still looked shocked.

"What made you come to the village?" Carlisle asked Lobrutto.

"There have been international phone calls made from the airport here. The girl was seen. It is not usual for a village girl to make such calls."

"Does the DGSE know what the calls were about?"

Lobrutto shook his head.

"Why should phone calls make you think we were here?"

"Lefay tell us to come. He make a guess. A good guess, I think."

"Okay." Carlisle turned to Martine. "Tell them I'm through with the questions. They can lock him up now."

The fishermen had understood enough of Carlisle's English to know the interrogation was over. Martine had barely begun to translate when they made their move. Before either Brennan or Carlisle could do anything, Lobrutto had been lifted from the deck and hurled bodily over the rail.

"Zac," Carlisle yelled. "The rope—grab the rope."

But there was no rope—just a severed end hanging limply in Brennan's hand. Now Carlisle understood what the buckets were for. He saw the men upend them, saw the contents slop out into the water—the fish heads, the guts and the blood—all of it streaming away in the dark, discoloring the wake behind the launch.

One of the men grinned at Carlisle, moving his hand to simulate the motion of a fin through water. The other man spat over the side, making the sign of the cross as he did so.

"Jesus." Brennan swallowed.

Martine was shouting angrily at the villagers in Tahitian. Both fishermen spread their hands, looking awkwardly at Carlisle.

"I'm sorry," Martine apologized. "I didn't know. I had no idea."

"Know what?" Carlisle remembered his conversation with Auntie Pau.

"One of these men is the uncle of the girl Lobrutto killed. The village elders sent him to do this."

The man who had made the sign of the cross spoke to Carlisle in French.

"He wants to know if you'll tell the police in Papeete," Martine explained.

"Tell him no." He paused. "Tell him it's done and finished."

Martine glanced at him. "You couldn't have done anything," she said.

Carlisle didn't answer. "Get the launch turned around," he said. "I want Zac on the other side of the lagoon in case the French decide to send a plane."

"All right." She touched his arm. "We know about the submarine now. We know everything. My father died for it. The Frenchman doesn't matter."

"Sure." He squeezed her hand. "We'll talk about it later."

When she had gone, Brennan rolled a cigarette and lit it. "You're not counting costs, are you?" he said. "Don't buy that crap about what Martine's father died for."

Carlisle shrugged. "If anyone deserved it, Lobrutto did." At this moment the Frenchman's death seemed inconsequential to him. And, if it should not have or if the justice had been too harsh, Carlisle decided he either didn't care or was beyond passing judgment on himself or anyone else. In the pass life was cheap, an uncompromising environment on the edge of the ocean—a place only for fishermen and the sharks they hunted for a living. More than anywhere he'd ever been—here, at night, adrift in the current—neither absolute right nor absolute wrong had any meaning.

"So what do you think about the submarine?" Zac interrupted his thoughts.

"I think the CEP knew they were in trouble at Mururoa two years ago when they started building it and yet they still carried on with their testing program. And I think that's sick. Planning to blame the Russians makes it sicker."

"I mean, what do we do?"

"Stop the bastards somehow. Find a way of exposing the whole thing—get some proof so people'll listen to us. With the right kind of pressure France will be forced to clean up the atoll no matter how much it costs. And if they can't find the money there'll be an international effort to do it for them. There isn't a country in the world that's going to stand by and watch half the Pacific be contaminated. Lobrutto said the CEP were going to use the submarine because concreting the caverns was too expensive. If that's right all it'll take is money. Lots and lots of money."

Swinging sideways in the channel, the launch was turning back, heading for the quieter water in the lagoon. Waves were slopping against the hull driving spray across the deck and cleaning away the last traces of blood from the upturned buckets.

"Once we transfer everyone off here onto the fishing boat you get this thing the hell away from here," Carlisle said. "I'll send someone to find you in a couple of days. Have you got enough food?"

"Plenty of cans on board." Brennan drew on his cigarette. "Don't worry about me. You're the one who'll need to be careful. If the DGSE suspect anything they're going to turn the whole goddamn village inside out."

"I know." Carlisle could see the outline of the waiting boat. "Here's our ride."

"Why don't you and Martine take a couple of guns with you?"

Carlisle shook his head. "That's not going to help this time." He called out to a man on the fishing boat and alerted Martine on the bridge.

"This has really turned into something, hasn't it?" Brennan was uncharacteristically thoughtful. "One hell of a deal. Here we are on some godforsaken Pacific island trying to stop the French government from pulling off one of the biggest hoaxes of all time. You, me and Martine against the French Navy."

Carlisle smiled. "We're doing pretty well so far."

"So far we didn't have a submarine to stop." Brennan grinned at him. "Old Daniel Tumahai didn't know what he was getting us into, did he?"

There was a bump as the launch drew alongside the boat.

Carlisle hurried to stop Martine who was preparing to disembark with the crew. Slung across her shoulders was one of the submachine guns.

"Leave that here," he instructed. "Zac's looking after the armament."

She handed the gun to Brennan in silence.

Carlisle followed her over the rail and jumped down

onto the deck of the boat. "See you later," he waved at Brennan.

"Yeah." Brennan returned the wave. Still smoking, he remained standing in the dark for some minutes watching the boat until it slid away behind the reef.

Lying uncomfortably on his back, Carlisle abandoned his attempts to sleep. Unlike nights in the fare at the village, here in the bush the air was oppressively hot and his head was pounding with the noise of surf beating outside the reef.

Martine had brought them to this place, prepared the bed of palm leaves and laid out the blankets they had carried with them from the village. In the moonlight it had taken them nearly an hour to reach their camp, an overgrown hollow close to the ocean on the island's northeast coast where they were far enough away from the beach to be safe from any ground search and screened from the air by the canopy of vegetation that was blocking his view of the stars.

He was wide awake now, remembering what Zac had said about counting costs, conscious of a jumbled collection of unwelcome thoughts hovering in the corner of his mind waiting for him to let them in—waiting for him to rekindle the image of Stephanie, for him to relive the violence at Wailuku and at the village, and for him to see again Lobrutto disappearing into the waters of the pass.

Zac was wrong. The costs of solving the puzzle had been too high. Today, directly or indirectly, he had been responsible for the deaths of four people—the guards, the girl and the man who had killed her. And for what? To learn he was capable of acting in a way he had previously thought impossible? To discover that a submarine was to be deliberately sunk in the lagoon at Mururoa? Or to prove that in embarking on a crusade of good he had sacrificed Stephanie and caused an innocent Tahitian girl to be raped and killed in front of her mother?

He began to sweat, gripping the blanket with both hands, trying unsuccessfully to justify a series of events over which he had never had control and which now were threatening to overwhelm him.

He reached out for Martine but when she came to him he could not speak. Her hands were cool on his forehead, he could smell the warmth of her, feel her body close to his, but still he could not explain.

"It's all right," she whispered. "It's all right."

"I can't stop thinking," he mumbled.

"I can make you." She sat up slowly, studying his face while she unfastened her pareu. "Don't try and think."

In the moonlight filtering through the leaves he could see her breasts, the curve of her throat and the outline of her face.

She leaned forward, brushing her lips across his mouth. "You don't understand," she whispered. "This night is just for us. For you and for me. Nothing else matters."

He experienced a sudden, vivid recollection, a memory of her standing in the lagoon at evening time with the sun in her hair, a picture of extraordinary clarity to remind him of how much he had wanted her then and how much he had always wanted her.

Gently, she took his hands and placed them on her breasts, waiting for him to respond. Her skin was burning, her mouth was slightly open, and her hair was falling across her face.

"Christ," Carlisle breathed. "You don't know what you're doing."

For an answer, she leaned forward again, pushing down against his palms until her face was close to his. "I do," she said softly. "Oh yes I do."

This time when her lips touched his, Carlisle kissed her, tasting the salt freshness of her, forgetting everything. She was squirming against him, breathing quickly, anticipating the moment when his hands would touch her between her thighs so she could cry out his name to claim him, to urge him on, to make him hers.

They made love quickly on the bed of palm fronds, two people brought together by a shared need and an unspoken sharing of themselves for themselves and for each other.

Afterwards, with Martine cradled in his arms, Carlisle slept, unmoving, untroubled and at peace.

It was not until early dawn that his peace was shattered by the arrival of the first helicopter.

NINE

FLYING in from the south, sweeping across the reef at tree-top level, the helicopter banked immediately above them, hovered for a moment, then turned toward the village. Through leaves disturbed by the downdraft from its rotor, Carlisle could see part of the fuselage.

"Damn," he said. "Where the hell did he come from?"

Martine shivered. "It's as though they know where we are." She pulled her pareu round her. "I didn't think they'd use a helicopter."

"Helicopters," Carlisle corrected her. "Here comes another one."

There were two more, approaching from the same direction at an equally low altitude. They were combing the reef, heading for the pass.

"Keep still," Carlisle instructed. He was worried that the combined downdraft might open up the canopy too far.

Martine was rigid in his arms, her eyes shut tight against the dust swirling in the hollow.

The helicopters passed each side of them, moving away slowly until the chopping of their rotors was drowned out by the surf.

"Those guys aren't messing about," Carlisle grunted. "I wonder how well Zac hid the launch?"

Martine pushed herself away from him. "They're gone," she said. "Stop worrying about Zac. He's not stupid, is he?"

"No." Her irritation had caught him by surprise.

"If you can stop thinking about Zac for a minute, maybe there's something you'd like to say to me."

"Good morning," Carlisle said cautiously.

"That's it?"

He was unsure of his ground, not at all certain what she wanted.

"That wasn't a dream last night. Or are you going to pretend it was, so you can just carry on as if nothing happened?" Her mouth was set firmly.

Carlisle hadn't seen her like this before. "I didn't know how you'd feel about things this morning," he said.

"Meaning what?"

"Nothing. Forget it."

"You mean you thought it might've been a one-night stand, don't you? If that's what you think, why not say so?"

"Look, I wasn't sure whether you had something going with Zac." He stopped wishing he hadn't begun.

"Oh." Relief showed in her face. "Oh, you stupid man." She knelt in front of him. "I'm sorry."

"I've seen how he watches you."

"And never once saw how I looked at you," she said softly. "It's taken all this time." She leaned forward and kissed him on the mouth. "You're crazy."

Carlisle felt as though his pleasure was not deserved—as though somehow he'd been guilty of betraying his memory of Stephanie.

"You're thinking again," she said accusingly.

He smiled at her. "We have to stay here until those helicopters leave the island," he said. "And they'll be around awhile. If I'm not allowed to think, I'll have to do something else."

She nodded. "But you can't do it without me."

He pulled her down on top of him. She was irresistible, too beautiful, too desirable. And if he didn't deserve her, why had this happened? Why was she here, kissing him, touching him, forcing him to think of nothing else but her?

They made love again, this time lingering—whispering and wondering—taking their pleasure slowly until the sun was high over the reef and, in the hollow beneath the trees, the air had become almost too hot to breathe. Only then did he release her, watching in silence while she put on her pareu and combed her hair without once taking her eyes from his.

The spell was broken soon enough. At eleven o'clock the helicopters returned, flying in formation, heading out to sea in the direction from which they had come.

Now the wait began, Carlisle thought. A forty-minute wait for news from the village if indeed news from the village would be received at all.

He stood up, reluctant to confront reality, not yet ready to think of the village, of Zac or the submarine. For a while he allowed his mind to drift, knowing that the need to address the future could not be put off but unwilling to accept the fact. Only slowly did his thoughts turn to the new and difficult problem of the submarine.

He was toying with an idea when the messenger arrived, a fresh-faced boy who appeared in the hollow as if by magic. He was about eight, dressed in jeans and a brightly colored shirt.

"*Ia ora na,*" Martine greeted him.

The boy smiled shyly. "I speak English," he said. "I come for you."

"Well, well." She took his hand. "Very good English."

"I am given this job because I have learned it."

"Did Auntie Pau send you?" she asked.

"I am to say all is okay." The boy studied Carlisle. "You can do karate?"

"No. I tell you what, though. When we get back to the village I'll make you a model of a submarine."

"What's this?" Martine was suspicious. "You didn't say anything to me. You haven't been thinking, have you?"

He grinned at her. "Only since the helicopters went away. I figured you could only stop me for so long."

"You want to bet?"

"Not when there's work to do. Come on, let's go and find out what happened."

Auntie Pau was waiting for them by her fare. She seemed pleased they were back and was clearly in good humor.

"So, you spend a warm night in the bush with the mosquitoes," she said. "Do you sleep?"

"Yes, we did, thank you." Martine poked her head inside the entrance to the fare. "But we didn't eat."

"You look for food? You think I make something for you? I have better things to do."

Martine smiled broadly. "It doesn't look like it. Oysters, pahu, papaya and vanilla. Are you having a party by yourself?"

"I fix it for the men who come in the helicopter." Auntie Pau burst into laughter. "But then I forget to tell them." She looked at Carlisle. "You are still angry with me about the Frenchman?"

"No." Carlisle shook his head. "I'm not angry." Auntie Pau's high spirits must mean the inquiry had passed without incident, he decided. "How did it go this morning?"

"They send three helicopters." Auntie Pau grew more serious. "You see them, I expect. One land here on the beach with men who ask many questions, but these are not men from the Direction Générale de la Sécurité Extérieure." She slipped easily into French. "Instead they are officers of the French Navy."

"What did they want?" Carlisle asked.

"What do you think? To ask about the launch, of course. Many people on the island see the flares from the pass and there are ships who receive the radio signals also. These officers believe the launch is sunk but I think they do not care very much. They say the men from the DGSE are, how you say it, cowboys, yes?"

The villagers had been lucky, Carlisle thought. The launch had probably been requisitioned from the navy. If it had, Lefay would have found himself in a difficult position.

"Did they ask about me and Zac?"

"They want to know if there are Europeans on the island who are not tourists," Auntie Pau grinned. "I say Europeans are shit."

"Is that all they wanted to know?" Martine was surprised.

"One man see the truck where it is being fixed up and say the work is very good but I think they are not suspicious. Then they look at the hole from the spear in the wall of the store. I forget about it. The hole is fresh with bright metal and no rust."

Carlisle had forgotten, too. "How did you explain that?" he said.

Auntie Pau spread her hands. "With the truth, of course. What else? I say a silly girl makes it yesterday with her spear gun and she is lucky not to hurt someone."

Carlisle grinned. "Then they went away?"

"Only after they talk to the other helicopters on their radio. I hear some of it. There is much wreckage from the launch along the east coast of the reef."

"Did you mention the whiskey?" Martine queried.

"A little. One man who fly the helicopter knows something of the pass, I think. He laughs and says to me he would not go through the pass in a boat at night even if he is sober. They are happy when they fly away. I am sure."

"Which is why you decided to fix a nice lunch for us," Martine said. "Auntie Pau, you are a lovely lady. I've never been this hungry."

"We send a boat for your friend Brennan now?" Auntie Pau asked. "With a green flag, yes?"

"I think we'd better," Carlisle answered. "I'll go too, though. Have you any idea how long it might take us to find him?"

"When we do not know where to search, four hours, maybe more. You must remember the lagoon is over seventy kilometers long and nearly thirty kilometers wide." Auntie Pau hesitated. "I think you not bring the launch back here. In case the helicopters come again."

Although Carlisle knew she was right, he was reluctant to scuttle the launch. The radio and the radar were potentially too useful to throw away and if the plan rattling around in his head was to stand any chance of succeeding, the radio could be invaluable.

"Okay," he said. "We'll leave the launch where it is. For the time being, anyway."

"That is good." Auntie Pau went into the fare. "You come for some lunch now. While we eat, you tell me what we are to do next and explain why it is that two young people who have spent a night in the bush should be so pleased with themselves."

Because Carlisle was not entirely sure what to do next and because he had no intention of confirming Auntie Pau's suspicions, he let Martine do the talking while he concentrated on the oysters and the wonderful portions of glistening blue tridacna clam. He ate steadily, enjoying being with Martine, half listening to her evade questions and half thinking about the submarine. When at length the meal was over Auntie Pau went to arrange for a fishing boat, leaving them alone in the fare.

"You'd better watch out," Martine giggled. "She thinks you've taken advantage of me."

"You make sure the record's straight by the time I get back with Zac." Carlisle's legs had gone to sleep where he'd been sitting on the floor. He straightened them carefully. "Are you sure you don't want to come with me?"

She shook her head. "I can't. There's the ceremony for that poor girl this afternoon. I have to stay."

"Okay. I'll be quick as I can." He kissed Martine before he stood up, unaware of Auntie Pau's presence behind him.

"The boat is ready." Auntie Pau handed him a folded green shirt. Her eyes were twinkling. "This is your flag. I am surprised you wish to leave again so soon."

"Yes. Right. Thank you." Carlisle retreated.

The boat was the same one that had brought Carlisle and Martine back from the pass. The crew members were familiar too—the two men who had thrown Lobrutto overboard last night. They greeted Carlisle sheepishly, pretending to be busy until the engine was started and the boat began moving off into the lagoon.

Once underway with the shirt hoisted to the masthead, Carlisle sat down comfortably in the cockpit trying to forget Martine so he could again concentrate on the problem of the submarine. Although he fell asleep twice and twice awoke with a start, annoyed with himself for wasting the afternoon, unconsciously he knew a single solution was beginning to show more promise than any of the others. The idea was crazy, he thought. But if they could pull it off—if they could afford to take the gamble on its working in practice—it was the answer to everything. It would depend mostly on how a model would perform, he decided. He would start building one tomorrow.

Carlisle continued thinking, wondering if a model was the right way to convince Auntie Pau to help them further and whether they should dare risk phoning again from the airport. He began worrying about details he had not previously considered, refining the plan as it became more complex, more complete and a good deal more dangerous.

Shortly after four o'clock, with less than a quarter of the

lagoon left to cover, the fishing boat entered a narrow strait between two motus. Practiced eyes told Carlisle the islands were geologically identical, looking as though they had once been joined together where the cliffs were higher and the coral was the same color—sister islands with inlets large enough to conceal a boat.

He'd already guessed this would be the place when the launch appeared. Traveling fast in a long curve around the island on his left, he saw it enter the far end of the channel. Zac was at the wheel, legs apart, balancing on the skeleton of the bridge.

If the fishermen were pleased the search was over they showed no signs of it. They throttled back the engine waiting for the launch to come toward them.

"Ahoy there," Brennan called. He switched off his engines, letting the launch slow itself. "Is that a green flag I see or is it your washing, Captain Carlisle?"

One of the fishermen threw out an anchor, leaving his companion to secure the bow of the launch while Brennan came aboard. "Well?" His expression was apprehensive. "What happened? Is everything okay?"

"Non-event," Carlisle said. "Three navy helicopters—no one from the DGSE."

"Thank Christ for that." Brennan was relieved. "I saw the choppers. Two of the bastards flew right over the top of here. If they'd come in from the opposite direction they could've seen me, I think. I picked them up on the radar—when they were about twenty miles out."

Carlisle was interested. "You got it going, then?"

"Sure. I picked you up too. It doesn't identify green shirts, though, so I had to wait."

"We're leaving the launch here," Carlisle said. "How long will it take to strip out the radio and the batteries?"

"I don't know." Brennan thought. "It's pretty easy. An hour."

"What about the radar?"

"Forget it. It's no use ripping that out unless we refit it properly on another boat and it'll take a hell of a lot of work and time."

"I still want to do it," Carlisle said.

"No, you don't. We don't have any time."

"What do you mean?" Carlisle was immediately worried.

"Because I didn't have much else to do I spent half last night playing around with the radio—tuning in to anything I could find. I tell you, the airwaves are real busy out here. Most of the signals I couldn't figure out—you know, coded stuff—but on a couple of frequencies there was some plain old voice communication. Even with my lousy French it wasn't hard to get an idea of what's going on." Brennan paused for effect. "The CEP are towing the sub into the Mururoa lagoon six days from now."

"Damn." Carlisle swore under his breath.

"Which means we'll have to move in a hurry if we're going to stop the bastards," Brennan said. "Six days isn't long. Not when we're stuck here on Rangiroa."

Carlisle was thinking hard. "We don't have to stop the submarine." He glanced at Brennan. "At least I don't think so. We just have to help things along."

"What are you talking about?"

"I'll explain later. I've got to build a model. Time's going to be the problem now. I never thought they'd move this fast."

"So what about the radar?"

"Leave it. We'll just salvage the radio."

Brennan prepared to reboard the launch. "What about this baby? Hide it again or sink it?"

"What do you think?" Carlisle was too preoccupied to care.

"It's pretty shallow around here. I can see us knocking a hole in the hull and having half the goddamn thing sticking out of the water when the tide goes out. I'll park it back up in the inlet. Those guys in the choppers never saw it, so why should anyone else?"

"Okay. I'll give you a hand with the radio." Once Carlisle had made certain the fishermen understood what was happening he followed Zac on board the launch and started work.

The job proved unexpectedly difficult. As well as having to feed cables from the batteries through a maze of conduits, the batteries themselves stubbornly refused to be withdrawn from their special gas-tight compartment in the engine room. Not until Zac resorted to brute force and the end of a crowbar did they manage to free them.

As a result, by the time the equipment had been transferred to the boat and the launch was again concealed in the inlet, the sun had set behind the motus.

The channel was dark when the fishing boat started on its return trip to the village—for Carlisle another evening spent afloat, another unwelcome reminder of the evening before. Now the reasons for them seemed less clear, as though the journeys had no purpose. He was tired, physically and mentally weary of trying to keep one step ahead of the French and, for the moment at least, rapidly losing confidence in his plan.

Martine awaited them on the beach. After saying hello to Brennan and greeting Carlisle with discreet if unmistakable warmth she accompanied them to their fare listening to Zac explain what he'd heard on the radio.

"We've got less than a week," Carlisle said. "A day less."

She frowned. "To stop the submarine from being scuttled, you mean?"

He shook his head. "No. To use it to scuttle the French."

"I don't understand."

"Nor do I," Brennan said. "He's working on some idea or other but he won't talk about it."

"I've told you why." Carlisle ducked into the fare.

"Yeah, yeah. We get to hear all about it after you've built this model, right?"

"Right." Carlisle reappeared carrying a pencil and a sheet of paper. "I'm starting tonight." He turned to Martine. "I need a decent piece of wood, half a dozen empty cans and enough light to work by."

"What about the store?" she suggested. "We can start the generator. Then you'll have electric light. The generator's only switched off because the freezers stay cold enough overnight, but we can run it for as long as you want. I know where there's an electric drill, too. Do you need a drill?"

"It'd help." Carlisle smiled at her. "So would tin snips or a pair of scissors. I wouldn't mind some company to make sure I don't go to sleep."

"You've got it," Brennan interrupted. "This I have to see. A geologist making a submarine with a pair of scissors."

Martine compressed her lips. "John asked me."

"Whoa." Brennan grinned widely. "The job's yours. I'm not rushing to stay up all night."

"You're staying up anyway," Carlisle said. "Someone has to listen in to our new radio. We might pick up more information. You know how to drive it so you listen."

Brennan was still grinning. "How come you get the company while I have to sit by myself decoding a whole bunch of French radio signals?"

"Geologists are lonely people." Carlisle was amused. "We'll get someone who can speak French to babysit you. How's that?"

"Okay, deal. If I pick up anything that sounds exciting I'll send the babysitter to get you at the store." Brennan studied Martine more closely. Since his arrival back at the village he'd noticed the change in her manner. She seemed more than usually protective toward Carlisle and there was a new easiness in the way she spoke to him. It was funny how things turned out, Brennan thought. Funny how in no time at all the most unlikely people reacted in the most unlikely ways. He was disappointed for himself but not surprised and even pleased for Carlisle—almost.

"Is there something the matter with you, Brennan?" Martine had noticed him looking at her.

"Hell, no. What would be the matter with me? I'm fine. I'll get the radio and find someplace to fix it up."

When he had gone Martine turned angrily to Carlisle. "Zac thinks it was a race," she said. "I don't understand how you can be friends with someone like him."

Carlisle had absolutely no intention of admitting he knew what she meant. "Race?" he said.

"To get me into bed."

"Oh."

"Don't you care?"

"No." Carlisle kept a straight face. "It was no contest and I won anyway." He grabbed her before she could hit him, holding her until she stopped struggling. "Are you going to get this stuff I want?" he said.

"I suppose so." She paused. "It wasn't a race."

"I know." He let her go. "I'll meet you at the store."

Daybreak at the beach was a special time for Carlisle. Often he had risen early by himself just to watch the first rays of sun wash the whole lagoon with light. This morning, though, his confidence regained, he was insensitive to the sunrise and he was not alone.

At the south boundary of the beach, grouped around a shallow rock pool, four people had assembled to observe the launching of the submarine. Perched on a rock Martine sat in silence beside an unshaven Brennan, both of them watching while Carlisle lowered the model into the water.

Steadying it, he called out to the young boy standing at

the other end of the pool. It was the boy who had collected Carlisle and Martine from their overnight camp, his expression one of studied concentration, a length of nylon fishing line held loosely in his hand.

"Gently now," Carlisle said. "Tow it out a little way."

With the exception of the bamboo periscope and its bean-can conning tower, from a distance the model was remarkably lifelike. Nearly three feet long, and apparently made of tin plate cut from other cans, it formed a small bow wave and trailed smoke from a handful of Brennan's tobacco smoldering in its conning tower.

"Right," Carlisle said. "Here is a clearly recognizable Typhoon-class, nuclear-powered Soviet submarine. The Americans and the Australians have seen it hanging around in the South Pacific, the French have been photographing it off Mururoa for several days and everyone knows what it is. At this moment it is also very obviously on fire."

"Whereabouts is it supposed to be?" Brennan asked.

"Just outside Mururoa under tow. The French have announced their intention to tow it into the lagoon to stop it sinking in two thousand feet of water outside the reef where recovery would be impossible. The French are being very responsible. TV crews are shooting the whole thing from the dock, from ships and maybe from a couple of helicopters so everyone can see for themselves how responsible they're being."

"You're enjoying this, aren't you?" Martine threw a lump of coral at him.

Carlisle had to admit he was, if only because he'd tried out the model secretly in the dark an hour ago. "Just watch," he said. "Don't forget it's being towed."

He called to the boy. "Pull the line slowly—just keep her coming toward you."

Surrounded in smoke, the submarine began to move. When it neared the center of the pool Carlisle joined Martine and Brennan on their rock. "What do you think?" he said.

"Great," Brennan answered. "We'll be able to sell this to the CEP. What happens now?"

"I'll show you. Remember what Lobrutto said—this is all being televised." Carlisle crossed his fingers, then gave his instruction.

At once the boy tugged sharply on the towline, snapping a loop of thin cotton that had been holding the nylon close to the bow. He continued pulling the model steadily across the pool.

Intrigued, Brennan saw that the line was still attached to the submarine, no longer at the bow but at a much higher point—to the periscope at the top of the conning tower. Now the pull on the towline was making the bow dip, creating drag at the front of the hull. Slowly the model began to change direction, swinging sideways until it took up a position at right angles to the line.

"Keep going," Carlisle shouted.

The boy reeled in more nylon. And as he did so the model began to tip, pulled over by its periscope. A second later the submarine capsized, exposing what lay beneath the tin plate superstructure—a smaller and more rudimentary submarine carved from a simple piece of timber.

"You bastard." Brennan was on his feet. "You clever old bastard. It's brilliant, bloody brilliant. This is going to make the French shaft themselves in front of half the TV cameras in the world. I like it. Boy, do I like it."

Martine was only slightly less restrained. She squeezed Carlisle's hand, appreciating now what he had labored all night to accomplish. Her eyes were sparkling. "It's tremendous," she said. "It worked perfectly—absolutely perfectly."

Despite the success of the demonstration Carlisle was more guarded, worried that their enthusiasm would evaporate when Zac and Martine started thinking about the practical difficulties in capsizing a full-size submarine weighing not a few pounds but thousands of tons.

"This is the only way we can handle something as big as a nuclear sub," he said. "Use the pulling power and the inertia of the ship that's doing the towing—make the French pull over their own damn submarine." He stopped. "I don't think you understand what's involved to make this work in real life. It's going to be as risky as hell."

"We can make it work," Brennan grunted. He was already thinking.

On the far side of the rock pool the boy had retrieved the model and refloated it in the shallows.

"I'll fetch Auntie Pau," Martine said. "You want to show her, don't you?"

Carlisle nodded. "I figure she'll be happier to help us if she understands what we're going to do. We need a boat to take us to the atoll for a start. Do you know how long it'll take one to get from here to Mururoa?"

"A long time." Martine frowned. "The fishing boats are awfully slow. Let's ask Auntie Pau. She'll know exactly."

"Hold on." Carlisle wasn't ready. "There're a couple of things we need to talk about first. Like who's going to do what." He began explaining, focusing on the details of how the towline could be linked to the conning tower before it was disengaged from the bow, a job that would have to be carried out while the submarine was under tow in front of hundreds of people.

Only half listening, Brennan was already absorbed with the problem. Like Carlisle, he knew there was all the difference in the world between a model in a rock pool and the real thing outside the lagoon at Mururoa.

"Martine's father had a photo of a Typhoon submarine in his press clippings," he said. "That's one hell of a big sub. There's only one way you can tow something that size—with a steel hawser."

"Zac, it's not a Typhoon-class submarine," Martine reminded him. "It only looks like one above the waterline."

"They'll still use a hawser." He paused. "And it'll be under a lot of strain, too."

"So how do we handle it?" Carlisle asked.

"I figure there'll be an eye at the end of the hawser. You make an eye by splicing the cable back on itself or clamping it back under a couple of U-bolt clips. One way or the other I reckon we'll be able to slip a hook round the towline that'll jam up on the splice or against the other bits and pieces. Then at the right time all we have to do is cut through the eye."

"You've lost me," Martine complained. "How does that connect the towline to the top of the conning tower?"

Brennan smiled. "I left out the easy part. Look, the eye of the hawser is slung over a bollard or something at the bow of the sub, right? So, as soon as I get on board I tie a bloody great rope around the periscope or whatever I can find on the top of the conning tower. Submarines have a whole bunch of pipes and tubes sticking out of them so I can't see that being a problem. I hook the other end of my rope onto the hawser ahead of the eye and we're in business. The minute I cut through the eye the French are buggered. They'll have a towline connected to the last place anyone would want. No matter how quickly they try to slow down they've had it. I abandon ship and watch them drag her over."

"What's all this singlehanded stuff?" Carlisle said. "What makes you think you're going to do this by yourself?"

"I've volunteered," Brennan answered cheerfully. "Anyway, you don't know how to cut through an eye on a steel cable—I do."

"How?"

"With a gas torch. The one I've been using on the truck."

"It'll take too long." Carlisle had a different idea.

"No it won't. The line'll break before I'm halfway

through." Brennan lit a cigarette. He threw the match into the pool.

"But you won't be able to get away," Martine said. "You'll be arrested—afterwards, I mean."

"Sure." Brennan grinned. "That's right—afterwards. In front of all the cameras, after they've shot pictures of a fake Russian submarine. I'll be an international hero overnight—Zac Brennan, the man who saved the South Pacific."

"Stop dreaming," Carlisle said. "Afterwards isn't the problem. Getting on board's the tough part."

"Wrong." Brennan refused to be put off. "I've worked at Mururoa, remember? I'll just arrange to have our little old fishing boat waiting at the dock and slip out at the right time. There's not going to be anyone on board a burning nuclear submarine to stop me, is there? That's one of the neat things about the idea." He grinned again. "You're being smart. You've already thought this through. It'll damn well work and you know it."

"Just testing," Carlisle smiled.

"I don't think it'll be hard to get on board," Martine said. "Zac's right. The French won't be expecting anyone to get near a submarine that's on fire, will they?"

"No." Though his main concern remained, Carlisle was encouraged. Because neither Zac nor Martine had come up with objections or uncovered any obvious flaws in the idea he was inclined to believe the scheme might not be so crazy after all.

"Do you really want to do this by yourself?" he asked Brennan. "What about your leg?"

"The leg's fine—good enough, anyway. And if you mean do I want any help, no, I don't. I'll have a couple of guys on the boat with me. They can give me a hand with the rope and the gas cylinders if I need it." He threw his cigarette away. "I'd rather you and Martine looked after things on shore. That's what you have in mind, isn't it?"

Carlisle nodded. "André Vincent said he wants to come out here so I'll tell him to get on a plane to Tahiti as fast as he can make it. I think we'll find out if Eva can organize something for us in Hawaii, too. She could leak the story to one of the newspapers in Honolulu—you know, explain what we're going to do. She could try the TV networks too, I suppose. That ought to guarantee us some friendly coverage. Martine and I can meet whoever's coming at Papeete and go out to the atoll with them."

"How the hell are you going to do that?" Brennan asked.

Carlisle didn't answer, his thoughts momentarily elsewhere.

Zac repeated his question.

"Fly," Carlisle said. "We'll be on internal flights so I don't need a passport. Seeing as how the DGSE have decided we're not here it'll be safe enough at this end and I can't imagine them watching any of the airports for us now—not when there are going to be foreign TV crews and journalists flying in from everywhere. The French have got enough to do without worrying about us."

"John," Martine said suddenly. "If you write the whole thing down we can fax André and Eva from the hotel. You can explain about the submarine—everything. Then all they'll need are photos of it happening."

"That's not a bad idea." Carlisle thought for a second. "How about getting someone from the village to send the faxes for us? You don't want to be seen making any more phone calls or sending messages."

"Auntie Pau will fix it." She stood up. "There's a lot to do, isn't there?"

"More than you think," Brennan said quietly. By avoiding any mention of Lefay and Soufrin when the possibility of returning to Papeete had been raised, Carlisle had given himself away. It was still there, Brennan realized. The dark side of Carlisle he didn't understand and one Martine didn't know existed.

The boy had tired of playing with the submarine. He carried it around the rocks and placed it carefully at Martine's feet.

"How would you like to pull it across the pool again?" she asked. "For Auntie Pau."

"It is no good," he said. "The tobacco is wet from when it tipped over."

She smiled. "Go and tell Auntie Pau we have something to show her while Zac puts some more tobacco inside for you."

His face brightened. "We do it once more only?"

"Yes. Then you can have it to keep."

Carlisle watched him run off toward the village, a barefoot boy who, with any luck at all, six days from now might see newspaper pictures of a full-size submarine which would bear a striking resemblance to his model.

As they had done to welcome their visitors, tonight the villagers had again gathered on the beach—this time to bid farewell to the fishing boat. Rows of burning torches lining the foreshore showed how many people now understood the importance of the mission and how many of them had come to wish Brennan and his crew Godspeed for the long haul to Mururoa.

At the water's edge, two fishermen were saying goodbye to their wives and families. Like Brennan, they too were volunteers, the same men who had been on board the launch two nights ago in the Tiputa pass. They waded on out to the boat, leaving Brennan to finish saying his own goodbyes.

After Auntie Pau had kissed him on both cheeks she handed him a parcel. "You be careful with your cigarettes, yes?" she warned. "You put this somewhere safe."

"What is it?" he asked.

Carlisle answered the question for her. "Half a dozen

sticks of dynamite," he said. "It only arrived half an hour ago. Auntie got it for me."

"Jesus." Brennan was astonished. "Where from?"

"There's an old guy in another village who makes a living blasting holes in the coral for sewage disposal on the island. He's got a truckload of the stuff. I thought it'd save you burning through the hawser."

"Be a damn sight quicker, that's for sure," Brennan said. "I'll still take the oxyacetylene cylinders, though. They're already on board. I'll use them for a backup."

"A fallback," Martine corrected him. "The French had theirs—we have ours." She smiled. "Zac, is the radio working all right?"

"Yeah, it is." Brennan pointed out to the boat. "We've strung an aerial right up the mast. It gives us real good reception on all the frequencies we're interested in. I figure once we get nearer to the atoll the French won't be able to sneeze without us knowing."

"What about the rope?" Carlisle said.

"I've got four hundred feet of it—big manila. It's strong enough, I think, but boy is it heavy." Brennan hesitated. "I've taken a couple of the machine guns—they might come in handy."

Carlisle frowned. "If the French find those on board afterwards they'll have a damn good idea where they came from."

"Okay. I'll dump them out at sea. What about the others?"

"I'll get rid of them." Carlisle stuck out his hand. "I'll see you in five days, then."

Brennan shook it awkwardly, anxious to be on his way but strangely unwilling to leave the village and his friends.

"Hey, Brennan," Martine said.

"What?"

"Remember when you were stuck on Mururoa that night? I said I'd changed my mind."

"About me not being as big a bastard as you thought I was?"

She smiled. "I think I was probably right."

"Yeah." He grinned at her. "In that case you'd better kiss me goodbye, hadn't you."

Standing on tiptoe she kissed him gently on the lips. "You still need a shave," she said.

"Yes, ma'am. I'll see to it." He saluted. "Hey, John. When you send that fax to Eva tell her I'll pay if she wants to fly out to Papeete."

"Okay." Carlisle lifted a hand. "Luck."

Brennan grunted, turned his back, then waded out to the boat and clambered on board. The water was very warm, he thought, and the stars were very bright. And he had not expected to feel this way.

The fishermen started the diesel, letting it idle while they stowed the anchor and lashed down some of the equipment.

"Come on," Brennan growled. "Let's go."

He waved at the crowd on the beach as the boat began to slip away, bound this time not just for the pass but for the open water outside the lagoon and for an island of a very different kind lying nearly eight hundred miles to the southeast of Rangiroa.

Until today, this had been an adventure for Brennan—a roller-coaster ride without any clearly defined end because the end was unimportant. He had started out for the ride alone, never questioning where it would take him or much caring whether there was to be an end. It had been a time of excitement, of danger and of change. But now everything was different, he realized. He had changed. He could feel it, comprehend it even. This was his chance, the chance for him to finish things, wrap up Carlisle's crusade and stick it to the French.

It was going to be a hell of an end, Brennan thought. One that old Daniel Tumahai really would have liked.

Methodically he began to roll a cigarette.

TEN

EVERY seat on the plane was occupied. In a hastily extended first-class section, French officials from the National Radiation Laboratory sat beside colleagues from the Atomic Energy Commission while a number of journalists were crouched in the aisle interviewing two elderly gentlemen from the Direction des Centres d'Essais Nucléaires.

As far as Carlisle could make out, the journalists were making little headway with their questions and upon being told to return to their seats by the flight attendant for the third time they started to disperse.

"Scavengers," André Vincent said disdainfully. "They want their stories written for them." He sat beside Carlisle, wedged into a seat barely large enough for someone half his size. André Vincent was not just overweight, he was enormous with several double chins and dimples.

"Do you know any of those guys?" Carlisle asked.

"One or two, by sight. The young man with long hair—he works for a science magazine in Paris." Vincent's English was excellent. "Please, tell me what is the flight time to Mururoa from Papeete."

"I don't know." Carlisle was nervous. He wished he

hadn't opened the conversation. "I haven't been to the atoll before." Leaning over the seat in front of him he tapped Martine on her shoulder. She swiveled around.

"How long before we get there?" he asked.

She inspected her watch. "We'll be on the ground just before twelve."

"I see," Vincent said. "So there will be plenty of time for us to locate a good place from which to photograph things. We shall have lunch first, perhaps."

Martine smiled at him. "Mururoa's a military installation," she said. "Controlled by the Centre d'Expérimentation du Pacifique. It's not the kind of place to get lunch—not in the way you mean. I suppose it might be different today, though, because of the visitors."

"And there will be no food on board the aircraft?"

"No." She laughed. "There isn't time. These are just shuttle flights. At any other time the planes are filled with workers."

This morning, instead of her *pareu* Martine wore an expensive suit and flat heels, and was indistinguishable from a dozen other women journalists on the aircraft. Her camera and the press pass clipped prominently to the lapel of her jacket identified her as a member of the Agence France Presse.

As well as bringing assorted photographic equipment that included three cameras and a powerful telescopic lens, it was Vincent who had supplied the passes—one for Martine and another for Carlisle. He had also advised Martine on her outfit and yesterday, in a shopping excursion to downtown Papeete, made sure Carlisle purchased the kind of clothes that any well-dressed journalist would wear on a trip to the South Pacific.

Though no one had given them a second glance so far, their disguises were not altogether convincing, Carlisle thought. He settled back in his seat, unable to relax.

They had arrived in Tahiti three days ago to meet Vincent and a team from Channel 9 in Los Angeles who had brought Eva with them. Eva had spent the best part of an afternoon with Carlisle, chattering nonstop while he attempted to bring her up to date with all that had happened. She had boarded the plane with them today still chattering and still confident that Zac would be at the atoll and that nothing would go wrong.

If anything was to go wrong, Carlisle thought, at least half the bloody world would see it. The whole of Papeete was bustling with excitement over news of the burning submarine. Local television stations had reacted with predictable enthusiasm, providing saturation coverage of the event on almost every news broadcast. The possibility of disaster had been seized on with equal enthusiasm by the environmental movement and had brought together groups like the Autonomie Interne and the Front de Libération de la Polynésie who were struggling for self-government.

In the middle of all the fuss, increasingly strong protests from the Soviet ambassador in France were being either ridiculed or ignored. Carlisle felt sorry for the Russians. Who could take seriously a denial which everyone in French Polynesia could see was nothing more than a laughable attempt by the Soviet Union to claim that their submarine had never been at Mururoa and to pretend that it was not now on fire outside the entrance to the lagoon?

For Carlisle and for Martine the media attitude had confirmed what they had always feared. The hoax was all but foolproof and, if for any reason Zac had been delayed or their plan failed, the French fallback strategy would be an unqualified success.

Where was Zac? Carlisle wondered. Making last-minute preparations at the dock? Or adrift somewhere in the Pacific with empty fuel tanks and a dead engine?

"Soon we shall land," Vincent commented. "We will see

your fishing boat from the air perhaps? You will recognize it when we fly over?"

"Maybe." Carlisle was thinking of all the other things that could go wrong. He had spent half of last night in his hotel room trying to decide whether he believed Zac could pull it off and the remainder of the night fielding questions from Eva's Channel 9 team. Although the men from L.A. would not have bothered to come all this way if they suspected a wild-goose chase, Carlisle had detected a skepticism that became more pronounced as the night had worn on.

If he hadn't known before, he knew now. If something did go wrong—if the submarine was towed uninterrupted into the lagoon—if the French got it that far without incident, once it was sunk no one would ever believe the accident was not what it seemed to be. Nor would anyone care.

Television and newspapers had identified the submarine as being one of the Soviet Typhoon class. There was no doubt, there could be no doubt because for the cameramen, the reporters and for the world at large there was no reason to believe it could be anything else. The subterfuge was too clever and from the very beginning the French had known they could not fail.

Martine spoke to him over the back of her seat. "I'm getting jumpy," she said.

"Think how Zac's feeling," Carlisle muttered. Now the no smoking and seat belt signs had come on, and passengers were straining to look out the windows, hoping to catch sight of the atoll. "André wants to know if there's any chance of seeing the boat on the way in."

"There might be. From the right-hand windows, just before we land. Look," she pointed.

Mururoa lay ahead, five thousand feet below, a smaller version of Rangiroa but without the ring of motus clustered inside the reef.

Acting on instructions from the ground the plane

banked, losing altitude and entering bumpier air as the pilot turned away from the atoll. Three other aircraft were stacked up waiting to land and the facilities at Mururoa were struggling to cope with so much unexpected traffic.

Carlisle spent the time with his nose pressed against the window hoping there might be a glimpse of either the submarine or the fishing boat, but the wing blocked the single opportunity he had and the plane landed without his having seen anything at all.

Martine shook her head slowly. She, too, had seen nothing.

The passengers were disembarking, pushing forward to the exit.

"Mr. Carlisle, I come with you." Eva had stopped by Carlisle's seat.

"Shh." He put a finger to his lips. "Don't use my name. Wait until we get off."

"Oh, yes." She was embarrassed, remaining silent until they were outside on the tarmac.

"I am very silly," Eva said to Carlisle. "I forget."

"It's okay," he said, smiling. "I don't think anyone was listening."

A row of military trucks was waiting to take arriving passengers to the dock. Although he was almost certain that the DGSE would have been forced to ease security on the atoll, as a precaution Carlisle boarded with Eva, letting Martine accompany Vincent on the one before.

By road the journey from the runway to the lagoon entrance took less than ten minutes but it was long enough to provide Carlisle with an impression of the installation. He was astonished, not just by the number of buildings and the size of the main base but more than anything by the overall scale of the operation.

Recalling Zac's description of the octopus at Giselle, he started looking for it. He located four of them, spaced unevenly along the reef in the distance and spotted the tops of two others protruding from the lagoon. The word *octopus* described them perfectly, Carlisle thought. Giant steel octopods the French could no longer afford to build and which, after this afternoon, they believed they would no longer need to build.

He climbed down from the truck to find Martine in conversation with a stranger. He was a swarthy, well-built man wearing boots, leather gloves and a hard hat.

"John," she called to him. "Come and say hello to Henri."

Carlisle went over to shake hands.

"I work with Taufa and Brennan at Giselle," Henri said.

"I know." Carlisle hadn't forgotten Zac's description of the French rigger.

"You come from Hawaii, like Brennan?"

"Yes, I do." He wondered if Martine had arranged for Henri to meet them and, if she had, how much she'd told him.

"So you work for Mademoiselle Tumahai?" Henri inquired.

Carlisle nodded. "Kind of."

"And you have seen the submarine?"

"No, we haven't," Martine interrupted. "Not yet. Where's the best place for us to go?"

"I take you but I will not stay. Until three o'clock I work day shift on one of the drilling barges."

Martine turned to Eva. "Eva, if you want to see where we're going you'll be able to fetch your television people. They might as well have a grandstand seat."

"This isn't a bloody ball game," Carlisle said. "Let's just get on with it."

Martine knew he was worried about Zac. She took his hand while they followed Henri toward a row of heavy dockside cranes.

Uniformed CEP personnel were everywhere. They were carrying side arms and walkie-talkies but were finding it hard to control people straying outside the designated viewing areas, a job being made more difficult by some of the more determined photographers.

Henri approached one of the guards, speaking to him briefly.

"Please, where is it we are to go?" Vincent asked. He was perspiring and struggling under the weight of his bags.

"There." Martine pointed between two warehouses. "You can see the reef on the other side.

Henri returned. "It is okay to watch from under the cranes," he said, "but you must not climb on them. There are some men who will make certain it is safe for you to be so close when the submarine is brought in."

"Why should it not be safe?" Vincent asked him.

"Because of radiation. They say the fire on board is now in the reactor room."

"They're not missing a trick, are they?" Carlisle said. "How long will it be, Henri?"

"Soon, I think." The Frenchman turned to leave. "I return to my barge now."

When he had gone Carlisle asked Martine if Henri knew what to expect.

"No." She shook her head. "He doesn't need to know. I just got a friend in Papeete to phone him here last night to say we were coming."

"Mr. Carlisle." Eva touched his arm. "Is it okay for me to tell the men from Channel Nine to come to the cranes?"

"Sure." He was anxious to move on.

"I come back soon." Eva hurried away.

"Who is this Hawaiian lady?" Vincent asked.

"She works for Zac." Carlisle didn't want to talk. "I'll explain later." He began walking but stopped in his tracks before he reached the side of the dock.

Henri's recommended vantage point afforded a 180-degree view of the lagoon entrance. It also provided Carlisle with his first sight of the submarine.

"Jesus." He was stunned by what he saw.

Floating low in the water a quarter of a mile out to sea was the immense hull of the largest submarine Carlisle had ever seen. Tumahai's photos had failed utterly to convey the true size of it. Smooth, black and over five hundred feet long it gave the impression of being invulnerable. Dirty smoke billowing from a hatch in the conning tower added to its wholly forbidding appearance.

Two tugs were playing jets of water on the hull—toy tugs, dwarfed by the enormous bulk of the Soviet visitor.

"It is very large, is it not?" Vincent had set up his tripod and was busy fitting the telescopic lens to his camera.

Martine was dismayed. Like Carlisle she had never believed the submarine could be so huge.

"How big do you think the real one is?" she said quietly. "The French one that's underneath, I mean."

"God knows." Carlisle was unable to imagine what it would take to capsize something of such monstrous proportions. He watched one of the tugs edge forward to nudge the submarine with its bow but could detect no obvious tendency for the hull to roll. The tug was pushing harder, lining the submarine up in the channel.

Unconscious of Carlisle's misgivings and absorbed by the picture in his viewfinder, Vincent was taking shots one after another. "If they use tugs all of the way, your idea will not work," he said.

Carlisle's heart sank. Not once had he considered the possibility. It was days ago that Lobrutto had said the French would tow the submarine—time enough for them to have changed their plans.

"John, it's all right." Martine dug him in the ribs. "There—look."

On the opposite side of the lagoon entrance a small naval frigate was pulling away from the dock. It was the right size, Carlisle thought. With sufficient power for the job but with a shallow draft so it could enter the lagoon. Turning out to sea it headed for the tugs.

He followed its progress until he was certain he had guessed correctly. The frigate was to be the towing vessel. "Okay, Zac," he whispered. "The bastard's all yours."

During the next hour, while the frigate maneuvered into position and the tugs fussed around the submarine, activity at the dock increased. Visiting VIPs were being brought around the reef by boat to join a number of navy launches that had drawn up to moor in front of the cranes, creating a general air of expectancy in the crowd.

Carlisle occupied himself by sketching a diagram of the fake submarine for the L.A. film crew who were beginning to voice their own doubts about the practicality of overturning something so big.

He was squinting through Vincent's telescopic lens, endeavoring to see where the towline was being connected, when he sensed the presence of someone close behind him. He turned around.

"Mr. Carlisle, we meet again." Lefay stood beside Soufrin, a slight smile on his lips. "May I inquire what brings you and Miss Tumahai here at the eleventh hour?"

For the briefest of moments Carlisle was in danger of acting involuntarily. Fists clenched, he stared at the Frenchman.

Lefay redirected his attention to Martine. "Perhaps you will answer my question, Miss Tumahai?"

"You talk to me, Lefay." Carlisle said. "How did you find us here?"

"For that I am afraid I can take very little credit." Lefay's smile remained. "You see, Mr. Carlisle, there is something you have never understood. The so-called Tahitian patriots recruited by Miss Tumahai's father are all known to us. They are watched routinely by my department—some of them for a period of over two years now. We knew Mr. Tumahai visited you originally in Honolulu, we observed

Mr. Brennan's exploits here on the atoll with interest and we were all but sure that you and Mr. Brennan had returned to French Polynesia for some reason. Yesterday we were alerted to the possibility of your visiting Mururoa to witness the salvaging of the submarine." Lefay reached out and flipped Carlisle's press pass with his finger. "You have a new job, I see. What a remarkably versatile person you are, Mr. Carlisle."

Carlisle said nothing. Standing close to him Martine was biting her lip, uncertain of what to do. Gradually Carlisle's reason returned. At any minute the submarine would be on its way and once that happened—as long as Lefay didn't know about Zac—there was nothing the DGSE could do to stop him.

A few feet away André Vincent had reached his own conclusion of what was going on. He concentrated on his camera, pretending to be uninterested.

"Mr. Carlisle, you are under arrest." Lefay glanced at Soufrin. "Take him and the girl to the launch."

"What the hell are you arresting us for?" Carlisle spat out the words.

"Despite information to the contrary I believe that until a few days ago you and Miss Tumahai were on Rangiroa. I wish to question you about that and I am anxious to discover the present whereabouts of Mr. Brennan. Those are reasons enough, I think." Lefay paused. "Mr. Brennan is wanted for killing a construction worker here on the atoll."

"Get lost," Carlisle said quietly. "Look around you, Lefay. Look at all these people. You're not arresting anyone."

In the distance the frigate had taken up the strain. Carlisle saw the hawser tighten and he could hear the engines throbbing.

"Brennan didn't kill that man," Martine said. "I did."

"Bring them to the launch." Lefay walked away, ignoring her.

Soufrin had produced a gun. He summoned two CEP guards to help him.

Martine looked helplessly at Carlisle.

He changed his mind. "They don't know anything," he said. "We have to stall—go with them. If it's going to happen it'll all be over in a few minutes."

Following Lefay to a small launch, the two CEP guards escorted them along the dock, remaining at the head of a gangplank while Soufrin pushed Martine and Carlisle on board. Lefay was on the bridge, speaking on the radio.

Lying crumpled in the bilges was the bloodstained body of Henri.

"Oh, dear God, no." Martine knelt down to check his pulse. White bone showed through his hair on one side of his skull and blood was still dribbling from his mouth.

The frigate was coming, laboring to gain speed with the submarine in tow behind it.

"You understand this is the solution to the cracks in the atoll?" Lefay inquired. "The answer you have tried so very hard to find."

"You only think it's the answer," Carlisle said grimly. "All this killing has been for nothing, Lefay. We know the whole thing."

"But of course no one will believe you." Lefay smiled. "Why should they?" He pointed at the approaching submarine. "It is a very good copy, do you not think so? Even the Russians must be impressed."

Their job done, the tugs had turned back, their crews lining the rails watching.

"Come on, Zac," Carlisle breathed. "Come on."

He saw it suddenly—a tiny fishing boat pulling out from a wharf on the far side of the channel, a green shirt fluttering gaily from its masthead.

Traveling at right angles to the towline on what Carlisle judged was a collision course, it was already moving fast. He saw it vanish behind the frigate, reappear in the gap between the two vessels and nearly tip over as it bounced against the bow of the moving submarine.

Now Lefay and Soufrin had seen it. Lefay was shouting urgently over the radio while, with his gun in one hand, Soufrin fumbled to start the engine with his other. In the wake of the frigate, the submarine was filling the channel, gliding past the spectators.

Digging her fingers into Carlisle's arm, Martine held her breath.

Through the smoke a solitary figure climbed the ladder to the conning tower, secured the end of a rope to the largest of three massive tubes protruding from it and returned quickly to the deck.

But Zac was not alone. Crouched at the bow where the towline was attached, one of the fishermen was busy.

Alerted by increasingly frantic signals from the shore and by his own observation of what was going on, the captain of the frigate was trying desperately to slow down. Water boiled from the frigate's stern.

Soufrin had started the engine. Casting off the mooring he shouted at Lefay, then opened the throttle wide.

As the bow began to rise, in one easy movement Carlisle lifted Martine and threw her over the side. Before Soufrin could level the gun, he dived overboard himself.

"There." Bobbing around in the wake, Martine pointed at concrete steps leading back up onto the dock. She swam over to them, helping Carlisle before she started climbing.

CEP guards were waiting at the top. Intrigued like everyone else by the drama taking place in the channel, they indicated only that Martine and Carlisle should remain where they were.

A puff of smoke from the bow of the submarine was followed by what sounded like a gunshot. At once the towline rose dripping from the water. It tightened, forming a long curve between the conning tower and the frigate.

Unaware of Lefay and Soufrin in the approaching

launch, Zac and the fishermen had reboarded the boat. Only when the launch was nearly on him did Zac see it. By then both Lefay and Soufrin were shooting—not at Zac and his crew but at the rope.

In horror Carlisle saw Zac jump back onto the submarine, struggling to keep his balance as the bow dug in and the hull began to swing sideways. Beneath each arm Zac held a submachine gun.

"Oh God," Martine whispered. "The guns—he kept the guns."

Firing from the hip when the launch was less than a hundred feet away, Zac shattered the windshield, killing Soufrin outright at the wheel. A second later, still traveling at high speed, the launch slammed into the side of the submarine, disintegrating in a ball of flame.

Swinging more rapidly, the submarine was tipping. For a moment there was a glimpse of Zac scrambling back into the boat. Then the big guns on the frigate opened fire.

At the same time that the fishing boat was reduced to matchsticks, the end came for the submarine. Carlisle's misgivings had been unfounded. On the surface the submarine was unstable, made top-heavy by thousands of tons of steel in its fake superstructure. Gracefully, with agonizing slowness it rolled onto its side, snapping the rope and continuing to roll like some dying, deep-sea creature until at last it floated upside down.

Gone was the illusion of the Russian submarine. In its place, surrounded by smoke and debris, a French submarine of the Agnosta class wallowed belly-up for the spectators, the cameras and the world to see. A plan to legitimize the poisoning of an ocean had been shown to be a conspiracy and, amidst all the carnage, the revelation was absolute.

A silence fell upon the dock—a long uncanny silence of understanding—a silence to mark the passing of men who had destroyed the illusion and shattered not just a conspiracy but the reputation and the honor of a nation.

EPILOGUE

FOR nearly thirty years the atoll had withstood the onslaught of the tests. It had accepted them, tolerated them and absorbed them until its core could resist the blasts no longer. Fractured and weakened, powerless to prevent the invasion of seawater, the atoll had surrendered. Below the reef and deep beneath the surface of its green lagoon all the caverns now were flooded.

And seeping upward from the caverns came the brine. Hot, radioactive brine permeating through the cracks, infiltrating a clay layer too thin to contain it and spewing finally into the sunlight where nearly five thousand men labored to halt the flow of poison.

Since the world had learned the truth four months ago, the drive to heal the atoll had been unremitting. Of seventy-four caverns, more than fifty were on their way to being sealed, the steel octopods straddling the surface above them multiplying almost daily as materials arrived in an armada of vessels berthing at Mururoa's crowded dock. American riggers worked with recruits from British and Norwegian North Sea oil platforms. French supervisors argued with Australian geologists, and laborers from the Pacific Islands sweated alongside exhausted volunteers from Japan and Indonesia.

Twenty-four hours a day the pumps forced concrete into the atoll—millions upon millions of tons to cement the cracks and replace the remains of the clay with a more permanent shield against the rising tide of brine.

Reacting to worldwide condemnation, for a month the French had met the cost, only agreeing to accept practical and financial aid when it became obvious that the Pacific nations would not trust the repair of the atoll to the French alone. Now, with United Nations funding, the future of Mururoa lay not with the French but with the people of Polynesia and with men and women whose children would live to see the atoll as it had been long ago—whole, unspoilt and once again at peace.

For one man and one woman the atoll would be a symbol of their own future and a reminder of the part they had played in the salvage of an island.

The reminder, though, would be for themselves, for their friends and for a tiny group of villagers on the island of Rangiroa. That Carlisle and Martine had survived was of little interest and of less consequence to a public more concerned with the hazards of radioactive contamination than with recognizing the people who had exposed the threat. Had Zac Brennan lived, he would have been disappointed at how quickly his heroism was forgotten.

For Carlisle the retreat to obscurity had not come soon enough. It had taken the combined efforts of Eva and Martine to deaden the bitterness that had accompanied the end of his crusade and still, months afterwards, there were times when he questioned whether the costs had been too great.

This morning was not one of those times. Feeling very much awake, Carlisle sat at the kitchen table, sipping his coffee, listening to the rain and the traffic noise outside the window. The Honolulu rush hour had begun early—probably, he thought, because of the rain. Once people expected jams they made the congestion worse by leaving home earlier than usual.

Taking his coffee with him he went to the living room to

conduct the test. On the wall facing the window hung Vincent's prize-winning photograph of the upturned submarine. Carlisle studied it carefully, waiting to discover what his response would be. Today there was none.

"You don't have to do that, you know." Martine stood in the doorway behind him. Her hair was loose and she was draped in the bedspread. "All you have to do is ask me how you're feeling. I could write a note for you each morning if you like—before you get up."

"You only think you know me better than I do," he said. "You don't really understand at all."

"Oh." The bedspread slipped to the floor.

"Another bribe?" He grinned at her.

She smiled. "That's not fair. I just want to help you make up your mind about the trip. We have to go sometime, otherwise we'll never decide whether we want to live here or on Rangiroa. You can't put it off forever. Both of us know we have to go."

To exorcise the ghosts, Carlisle thought.

So we, too, can be at peace.